Nancy Drew®
in
The Clue in the Old Album

D0550288

Nancy Drew Mystery Stories® in Armada

For contractual reasons, Armada has been obliged to publish from No. 51 onwards before publishing Nos. 38–50. These missing numbers will be published as soon as possible.

Nancy Drew Mystery Stories®

The Clue in the Old Album

Carolyn Keene

Armada

First published in the U.K. in 1974 by
William Collins Sons & Co. Ltd, London and Glasgow
First published in Armada in 1985 by
Fontana Paperbacks,
8 Grafton Street, London W1X 3LA

Second impression 1987

Armada is an imprint of
Fontana Paperbacks, part of
the Collins Publishing Group

Printed in Great Britain by
William Collins Sons & Co. Ltd, Glasgow

CONTENTS

" One of Mrs Struthers's stolen dolls!" Nancy exclaimed.

·1· *A Stolen Handbag*

THUNDEROUS applause echoed throughout the crowded concert hall of the River Heights Museum of Art.

Nancy Drew, attractive in a white evening dress, joined in the enthusiastic tribute to Alfred Blackwell, the noted violinist.

"Oh, Dad, isn't he marvellous?" she whispered to her father, who was sitting beside her. "That gypsy music he just played——"

The artist returned to the stage and tucked his violin under his chin. As he began the melody again, Nancy was startled to hear a stifled sob from a white-haired woman who sat across the passageway. She was listening with rapt attention and tears rolled down her cheeks.

Nancy also saw something else. A dark-haired man on the end seat next to the woman was reaching over for a jewelled handbag which lay unguarded in her lap. Slyly he dropped it into his pocket, got up, and started quickly for the foyer.

"Dad, that man stole a handbag!" Nancy whispered excitedly. "I'm going after him!"

Before Mr Drew could recover from his surprise, she had scrambled past him and was hurrying up the passage after the thief. Turning his head slightly, the man saw Nancy and instantly guessed from her grim expression that she meant to stop him.

The pick-pocket's step quickened to a half-run. Pushing past an usher, he fled into the foyer. Nancy reached there only a moment later, but he was out of sight.

Doorways opened in three directions to various exhibition rooms. Choosing the nearest one, the girl ran down the corridor. The only person in sight was a watchman.

"Did a man in evening clothes come this way just now?" she asked excitedly.

"No one's been through here in the past twenty minutes, miss."

"He stole a jewelled handbag! Oh, please help me catch him!"

"You bet I will!" exclaimed the guard.

While he went one way Nancy chose the only unexplored corridor. Rounding a turn in it, she suddenly saw the thief far ahead. He had paused, apparently to examine the bag.

"Drop that!" Nancy cried out, starting towards him at a run.

The man hesitated. Then he pulled out the contents, flung the bag away, and darted through a door opening into an alley.

Nancy snatched up the bag, then resumed the chase. The alley was dark and the girl could see no sign of the man. Disappointed, but knowing it was hopeless to go on, she turned back.

From the entrance foyer came the sound of voices. Among a group of people Nancy saw the guard. Behind him were her father and the elderly lady whose bag she had retrieved. Upon seeing the bag in Nancy's hand, the woman exclaimed:

"Oh, I'm so thankful you recovered it!"

"I'm sorry the thief escaped," Nancy said.

"It doesn't matter, my dear," the woman replied. "As long as I have the contents of the bag that's all I care about."

"I'm afraid he took them," said Nancy. Handing over the bag, she explained what had happened.

Nervously the woman opened the bag. It was empty!

"Oh, my money is gone! And a letter and a photograph which mean a great deal to me!" she cried.

"I'll call the police," offered the guard, starting for a telephone.

"No!" the woman spoke up quickly. "Thank you, but I do not want any publicity."

Mr Drew spoke up, saying the authorities definitely should be notified. "No thief should be allowed to go free," he said.

"Very well," the woman agreed reluctantly. "I suppose the report must be made in my name. I am Mrs John Struthers of Kenwood Drive."

Mr Drew asked if she could identify the pick-pocket.

"I scarcely noticed him," she confessed.

"He was about thirty-two years old," supplied Nancy. "Dark, with a mottled complexion and piercing black eyes. He walked with a slight stoop and wore evening clothes too large for him."

"You're observant, miss," the guard said. "Come to think of it, I know a fellow who looks like that. Let me see—it must 'a been when I was janitor down at the bank. Yes, that's it."

"He didn't *work* there?" Nancy asked, amazed.

"No, he used to come in to see one of the tellers. They got mixed up in some crooked scheme together. The teller was fired. I don't know what happened to his buddy, but I heard he was a professional pick-pocket."

"How long ago was that?" asked Mr Drew.

"Six months or more. Well, I'll phone the police."

Mrs Struthers recalled that as she and her granddaughter were coming into the concert hall a man had stayed very close to them and had seated himself next to her.

"He probably noticed your bag, and planned all the time to steal it," Nancy surmised.

"No doubt," replied Mrs Struthers. She had regained her poise but a faraway look had come into her eyes. "If it hadn't been for that gypsy music——" She broke off as if she regretted having revealed something. Turning to Nancy, she added, "I am very remiss. I haven't even thanked you for all your trouble, and I really am most appreciative. May I know your name?"

"Nancy Drew," the golden-haired, blue-eyed girl replied, smiling. "And this is my father," she added, looking at tall, handsome Carson Drew.

Mrs Struthers turned admiring eyes on them, then said to Nancy, "I see now why it was you who happened to spot the thief. You are often spoken of in glowing terms for your cleverness in apprehending unscrupulous people."

Nancy laughed, brushing aside the compliment. She asked Mrs Struthers if they could be of any further help to her.

"I believe not, thank you," the woman replied. "I must find my granddaughter Rose. We have been invited to Madame Mazorka's reception for Mr Blackwell, but I hadn't planned to go, on account of Rose."

"You really shouldn't miss it," Nancy said kindly, thinking the social affair might take the woman's mind off her loss. "Perhaps——"

Nancy's remark was cut short by a girl about eleven years of age who unexpectedly pirouetted among them. She was strikingly pretty. Coal-black wavy hair fell to her shoulders and her cheeks were highly coloured. Dark eyes sparkled brightly, though they looked as if they were capable of blazing with temper.

Catching the girl's hand, Mrs Struthers said, "I should like you to meet my granddaughter. Rose, this is Mr Drew and Miss Nancy Drew."

"Hello!" beamed Rose, finishing her dance with a pert curtsy. "Wasn't the recital super?"

Nancy grinned at Rose's sprightly greeting. "Hello, Rose. Yes, it was, and I'm thrilled that we're going to Madame Mazorka's to meet the artist."

"We've been invited, too, so we can all go together!" Rose declared.

"Please, dear," remonstrated Mrs Struthers. "Perhaps the Drews have other plans. We can call a taxi."

"We should be delighted to have you travel with us," Mr Drew assured her, though he looked askance at Rose. "I'll get the car."

Without waiting for the others, Rose went along with him and hopped into the front seat. While she chattered gaily with Mr Drew, Mrs Struthers, in the back with Nancy, presently confided to the girl that she would like her assistance in solving a mystery.

"I'd love to help you," Nancy said, her interest awakened at once.

"Would it be possible, my dear, for you to come to tea at my home tomorrow afternoon?" Mrs Struthers asked eagerly. "I'd like to talk to you privately about it."

Nancy accepted the invitation. There was no chance for further conversation because the car was pulling up in front of Madame Mazorka's home.

The charming hostess was known in the community as a patron of the arts, particularly music. Attired in a gown of flowing grey chiffon, she received her guests graciously.

"Eet ees a pleasure to see you, Mrs Struthers, Mr Drew and Miss Drew," she greeted them. "You have enjoyed ze recital, yes?"

She introduced them to the violinist. As he shook hands with Nancy, Alfred Blackwell's eyes twinkled. "You are the young lady who was carried up the hall by my last encore, are you not?" he asked teasingly.

"That's a very kind way of looking at my interruption," she replied, laughing. "I wish I'd been as skilful in my performance as you were in yours."

As Nancy was telling the artist she hoped she would have the pleasure of hearing him play again soon, Rose suddenly pushed forward. "How about me? Don't I count?"

She shook hands with Alfred Blackwell, then spun away, twirling dangerously close to a portly gentleman who was trying to balance a plate of sandwiches and a glass of punch in one hand. To the strains of a three-piece orchestra she began to dance in the middle of the floor.

Many of the guests were staring coolly at Rose's flippant behaviour. Nancy realized that the best way out of the awkward situation would be for the girl to depart. She turned to the distressed grandmother.

"I believe my father is ready to leave now, Mrs Struthers," she said. "We'll be glad to take you home."

The woman was greatly relieved to escape and retrieved Rose. After the Drews had left them at their residence, they drove at once to their own attractive home, set well back from the street among flower gardens and trees. Nancy told her father of Mrs Struthers's invitation to talk over a mystery.

"Have you any idea what it might be?" she asked him.

"I've heard very little about Mrs Struthers," the lawyer said, "although I can see she knows how to pick a good detective," he added, smiling at Nancy. "I understand she and her granddaughter have lived in River Heights for two years. She's reputed to have been wealthy and travelled a lot, but it's said she now stays at home all the time. She's sad and very secretive about her affairs."

"It should be an interesting case," Nancy said reflectively. "I wonder if it could have anything to do with Rose."

"That child should be taught to behave better," Carson Drew declared, frowning.

"Maybe her actions are the result of pent-up energy," Nancy ventured. "Who knows, she may have some great hidden talent!"

"Perhaps you're right," said the lawyer, smiling. "Anyway, Nancy, until we know more about the family, I'd prefer you not to go to their house by yourself. Take one of the girls with you."

Consequently, the following day as Nancy drove in her convertible to the Struthers' home, she was accompanied by one of her best friends, George Fayne. George, a slender, boyish-looking girl with close-cropped brown hair, was as excited as Nancy over the prospect of a new mystery.

"You're sure Mrs Struthers won't mind your bringing me along?" she said.

"Quite sure," Nancy replied. "I telephoned this morning to ask her, and told her you always help me on my cases."

The car came to a stop in front of a large brick house, which stood at some distance from the others in the neighbourhood. It was surrounded by lawns and a high iron fence.

The two girls started up the long walk to the front door. Suddenly a shout behind them made them turn.

Too late!

Before they could tell who or what was coming at them, Nancy and George were knocked to the ground!

· 2 · *The Doll Collector*

"Whew!" breathed George, scrambling to her feet and rubbing her knee. "Where'd the cyclone come from?"

Nancy, shaken, and surveying her dusty skirt, was up already. She pointed down the path where Rose was precariously jerking to a halt on a bright red motor scooter.

"There's our trouble!" Nancy exclaimed.

Rose hopped off the scooter and with a graceful skip came towards them.

"Jiminy crickets!" she exclaimed. "When you get up speed on that thing, it's hard to stop." Then as an afterthought she added, "I'm sorry if I hurt you."

Nancy assured the girl that fortunately both she and George were all right, and introduced Rose to George.

"Aren't you a little young to be riding around on a motor bike?" George asked.

"Ordinary bikes are too slow," Rose declared. "I swapped mine with a boy for this scooter, but it doesn't work properly."

"Does your grandmother approve of your having it?" Nancy asked.

"Granny doesn't approve of anything I do," Rose pouted; then she laughed. "She couldn't do anything about the scooter. I traded my bike for the second-hand scooter before she could say no."

"Your name ought to be Wild Rose," said George, disgusted.

Rose frowned. "You're a meanie. You're a girl and they call you George!"

"Have you a licence for the scooter?" George asked.

Rose's face grew red. "No."

"Then it's against the law to ride it."

"I'll watch out for the police," giggled Rose. "Say, did you come to see Granny?"

"Yes, she invited us to tea," Nancy answered.

"Well, don't let her get you into her clutches—not with all those funny dolls of hers!" Rose warned.

Before the girls could ask what she meant, Rose ran off round the house.

"You heard what she said?" George asked in a hushed voice. "Maybe we're heading straight for trouble!"

Nancy nodded but did not offer to turn back. Always fascinated by an intimation of something unknown or mysterious, she had, in the past, become involved in many exciting adventures. Friends often declared that her ability to find the key to a baffling enigma was partly because she was a "chip off the old block," referring to her brilliant father.

The young amateur detective had won wide recognition by solving *The Secret of Shadow Ranch*. After that had come many other cases. Only recently she had cleared up *The Clue of the Velvet Mask*.

Nancy was quick to divide the credit for her successes with various friends. Now, as she rang the bell of the Struthers' residence, Nancy was glad that George was along to share what she sensed was to be an unusual assignment.

"How nice to see you again, Miss Drew," Mrs Struthers greeted her, as she opened the wide door. "And this must be the friend of whom you spoke. Come right in."

"Yes. I'd like to present George Fayne, Mrs Struthers. Do just call us George and Nancy, though."

"Thank you, my dear." Mrs Struthers was pleased. "How do you do, George?"

George acknowledged their hostess's greeting as the girls were led into a tastefully decorated living-room. There were several bowls of flowers attractively arranged and a silver tea service had been set out on a finely carved antique table.

Although eager to hear about the mystery of which Mrs Struthers had spoken the evening before, Nancy restrained herself from bringing up the subject. "Rose mentioned something about your dolls as we were coming in," she said. "Do you have a collection?"

"Does she!" cried Rose, who popped in the door and was obviously relieved that Nancy had made no reference to their collision. "Jiminy crickets, there are hundreds of dolls!"

"Rose, dear, don't shout so," Mrs Struthers remonstrated quietly.

Turning to Nancy and George, she told them that collecting dolls had been her hobby for the past few years and that she had acquired them from nearly every country in the world.

"Perhaps you'd be interested in seeing them," she

offered. "There's a great deal to be learned from dolls even after we have given them up as playthings."

"Why is that?" inquired George, who had seldom played with dolls.

Mrs Struthers, leading the way down a long hall, explained, "One can learn a great deal about people of other days and other countries from dolls."

Nancy caught her breath as the woman pushed open a door. Straight ahead against one wall of a large room was a tremendous rosewood cabinet with glass windows. On the shelves stood and sat Mrs Struthers's collection of dolls.

"How perfectly lovely!" exclaimed Nancy. "You must have some real treasures here."

Mrs Struthers reached into the cabinet and selected a little old lady, dressed in a red cape and black silk bonnet. Over her arm was a tiny basket.

"I have been fortunate in getting some unusual dolls," she told her guests. "This is one of the original pedlar dolls made in London in the nineteenth century. Notice the contents of her basket."

The girls were fascinated to see many miniature objects, including musical instruments, ribbons and laces.

"Oh, look!" marvelled George. "There are even little pots and pans!"

"And can you imagine making something like this!" Nancy exclaimed. She reached into the basket and picked out a tiny set of knitting needles holding a half-completed sock.

Just then the girls' attention was diverted by the sound of a tinkling melody. Rose motioned towards a small table where a beautiful doll stood on a velvet-covered box from which music was coming.

"Watch!" she directed.

The doll began to move her head from side to side in time with the music. To add to her charm, she brought up one hand to smell a wee bouquet of flowers she was holding, while with the other she demurely waved a tiny, jewelled fan.

"She's a darling!" Nancy exclaimed.

Mrs Struthers was delighted by her visitors' amazement, but suggested they return to the living-room now and have tea.

"Not for me," sang out Rose and left them.

"I'm afraid I have very little control over my lively granddaughter," lamented their hostess as she poured the tea. "Perhaps it's because of her heritage on her father's side."

Noticing Nancy's puzzled expression, she went on, "I feel I can tell you girls about this without fear of your violating my confidence. You see, Rose's father was a very talented violinist. Also, he was a gypsy, and gypsies, as you know, do not live as conventionally as we do. My daughter became entranced with him and his exquisite playing, and against Mr Struthers's and my wishes left home to marry him."

Listening absorbedly, Nancy now understood the reason for the woman's tears at the recital. "It must have been quite a shock to you," she said.

Mrs Struthers nodded. "We were greatly upset by my daughter's act and, I regret to say, rather harsh with her. She was banished from the family. When Rose was eight years old her gypsy father deserted them, and we pleaded with Enid to come home with her child."

"They did?" George asked eagerly.

"Yes, but too late. My daughter was in poor health and heartbroken besides. Within a few months she died. Three months later, my dear husband passed away."

"I'm so sorry," murmured Nancy sympathetically.

"Rose is now my problem," the woman confessed. "She is not aware of her gypsy blood, for her parents lived apart from the tribe and never told her. Naturally, I never have breathed the truth.

"My granddaughter is very headstrong. She doesn't

study in school, and runs off whenever it suits her fancy. If I leave her with adults or other children, she disgraces me by the things she says and does."

"Perhaps if you took Rose away for a year," Nancy began, but Mrs Struthers shook her head.

"We did travel abroad for many months but that only seemed to arouse the sense of wanderlust and freedom in her. Personally I enjoy travelling, and it gives me an opportunity to collect dolls.

"Collecting them means everything to me," Mrs Struthers continued. "You see, I have been searching for one particular doll. Now I must give it up, but I want you to continue the search. You will be given plenty of money to do it. But I shall not be satisfied until I find the doll."

"Is it a rare one?" asked Nancy, intrigued by the assignment.

"Yes, the doll is connected with Rose's past. If I tell you my secret, you must never repeat it to her."

Nancy and George said they would respect the woman's wishes.

"When my beloved daughter lay on her death-bed, she talked half deliriously about a doll. Almost her last words were, 'The doll! It's gone! Oh, Mother, you must find it for Rose.' "

"What did she mean?" asked George.

"I tried to find out, but Enid was too ill. I thought she said, 'Important. Very important. Clue——' "

At this instant a piercing shriek filled the air. Nancy was on her feet immediately and ran outside in the direction of the sound, followed by George and Mrs Struthers.

They saw a car driving away from the house with Rose half in, half out of one of the doors, which was open. She was struggling with a woman in the back seat!

· 3 · *An Assignment for Nancy*

"Nancy!" cried George. "Mrs Struthers has fainted!"

"Take care of her," Nancy directed quickly. "I'm going after that car."

She dashed to her convertible, intending to chase the other car. But it was unnecessary. Before she could start the engine, Rose had fallen to the side of the road. Nancy jumped out of the car and raced to her.

"Are you hurt?" she asked anxiously, as she picked up the girl, who was shaking convulsively. "What happened?"

Clutching Nancy tightly, Rose seemed more frightened than harmed. "I'm—all—right, I think, but I don't ever w-want to see those aw-awful people again," she sobbed hysterically.

Nancy realized the girl was so overwrought that it would be hard to get a clear account from her of what had happened.

"Had you ever seen them before?" she queried.

"N-no, they just stopped in front of the house and asked about Gran's d-dolls. I told them to come in, but they said no, we had callers."

"Then what happened?" Nancy kept her voice calm.

"The woman said it would be better if I brought out one of the rare dolls, so I d-did. When I held it up to show her, she grabbed it. I tried to get it back, but just then the man started the car, and I was half in it!" she shuddered.

"There, there, Rose, you're all right now," soothed

21

Nancy, "although you did have quite a fall. Try to tell me what the people looked like."

"They were awful mean-looking, and the woman had funny red hair. I never thought they'd steal Gran's doll."

"Which doll was it?" Nancy asked.

"The one on the music box, holding the fan," Rose said as Nancy led her back to the house.

Mrs Struthers, now revived, was pathetically relieved that her granddaughter was safe. "Oh, my dear child!" she exclaimed and hugged Rose. "Are you all right?"

"I'll be okay in a jiff, Gran," Rose told her, wriggling out of the embrace.

"What happened?" Mrs Struthers asked weakly.

Nancy related Rose's story. "Thank goodness you were here, Nancy," Mrs Struthers said fervently. "And you too, George."

Although the woman was exceedingly concerned over losing one of her precious dolls, she protested when the girls suggested notifying the police. She told them she wished to avoid any more notoriety.

"I'd prefer having you help me, Nancy," she said. "If you'll come tomorrow, I'll tell you the rest of my story."

By this time, Nancy was more intrigued than ever with the case. "I'll be here," she promised.

At dinner that evening Nancy told her father about the happenings of the afternoon. "The thieves got away in their black saloon," she said regretfully, "and the licence plate was so smeared with mud I couldn't read it. But I did notice that the car was the same make and year as mine."

"A slim clue," observed Carson Drew, "but I know you'll make the most of it."

"I've promised to help Mrs Struthers," Nancy smiled. "Rose needs help too. She's rude and undisciplined, but I think with her musical heritage she'd improve under some sort of artistic training."

"I'm afraid it will take a good bit of training," declared Mr Drew.

The next day, Nancy was about to leave for Mrs Struthers's home when her friend Bess Marvin arrived. Attractive and plump, Bess was just as feminine as George Fayne, her cousin, was tomboyish. She was brimming with the news that the River Heights Yacht Club was holding a meeting that afternoon for the older girls. An important announcement had been promised.

"Maybe what you've been hoping for about the sailing races is coming true, Nancy! I mean, letting the girls race. Grab a scarf and let's go."

Nancy shook her head. "Sorry, Bess, I can't make it."

"You're going somewhere with Ned Nickerson!" her friend teased.

"No."

"Then you're on the trail of another mystery!"

"Well, perhaps," laughed Nancy. "Hop in the car and I'll drop you off at the club, but I can't stay myself." On the way, Nancy brought Bess up to date on her new case.

"How I'd love to see those dolls!" sighed Bess as they pulled up in front of the yacht club. "I imagine some of them have gorgeous clothes."

"They do," said Nancy, and promised to take her to the Struthers's home soon.

She drove on alone, and upon reaching the house found that Mrs Struthers had sent Rose to visit a neighbour so that she could talk to Nancy without interruption.

"You missed the most important part of my story yesterday," the woman began in a quiet voice. "I believe I was just telling you my daughter's dying words when those people . . ."

"Yes," said Nancy understandingly. "You mentioned something about a clue."

"A clue which I've tried unsuccessfully to find," lamented

her hostess, "though I think it may be here. Perhaps you can detect it."

Unlocking a cabinet, she removed a thick book. It appeared to be an old family album, covered with handsome brass filigree work and studded with precious stones of various colours.

"This is a very valuable possession," Mrs Struthers explained, "and is filled with family photographs."

"How does it tie in with the clue?" queried Nancy.

Mrs Struthers sighed. "As my daughter lay on her deathbed, she seemed worried about Rose's future. She tried desperately to tell me something. Her last words were: 'Clue in . . . the old album.' "

"In this one, you think?" asked Nancy, turning over the pages of the photograph album.

"I'm not sure," replied Mrs Struthers, as Nancy stopped at a picture of a pretty child of eight or nine holding a doll. "That one is my daughter Enid when she was a little girl," the woman said, wiping away a tear. "And here is a picture of her in her wedding dress."

"Your daughter was beautiful," said Nancy. "And the dress is lovely."

"I never saw it," Mrs Struthers sighed. "Enid bought the dress herself and later when she needed money, she sold it. After she returned home, broken and heartsick, she slipped this picture into the album. I found it after her death."

"What was her married name?"

"Pepito . . . Mrs Romano Pepito. But Rose goes by the name of Struthers."

"Your daughter's final words were 'The doll! It's gone! Find it for Rose,' " Nancy said. "Could she have meant the doll she holds in the photograph of herself as a child?"

"I thought so at first, but that doll is here in the house. It gave me no clue."

"Apparently the lost doll holds a secret to something that would mean a great deal to Rose," mused Nancy.

"Exactly," agreed the grandmother. "Rose may have a fortune hidden somewhere for her."

"You've searched the album thoroughly?"

"Dozens of times. But perhaps your young eyes might detect something I've missed."

Nancy was eager to examine the album.

"It's possible my daughter didn't mean this album," Mrs Struthers remarked thoughtfully. "She may have intended to tell me the all-important clue was hidden in an album belonging to the Pepito family."

"Have you talked to any of them about it?"

"No, indeed! Searching for a gypsy tribe would be an almost hopeless quest. Romano's people may be wandering anywhere on the American continent."

"Can Rose explain what her mother meant?"

"She knew almost nothing about the Pepito family. My daughter was careful tó keep such information from her. Enid told me very little. While she was here she scarcely mentioned her husband's name, although I know she thought of him constantly."

During the next hour, Nancy carefully went through the album with its interesting photographs. She could find no clue which appeared to have any bearing on the mystery.

"If we only had some hint about the doll your daughter meant," said Nancy. "Even knowing if it had been misplaced, or perhaps sold, would help."

"I rather doubt either of those possibilities," replied Mrs Struthers.

"It may have been stolen," ventured Nancy.

The elderly woman hesitated. "There is something rather ominous that may be connected with the doll's disappearance," she confessed. "The jewelled album contained a note written in a strange hand. I was afraid Rose might see it some day and ask questions about her past, so I destroyed it."

"What did the paper say?"

"I can never forget the words," Mrs Struthers spoke slowly. "The message was this:

" *'The source of light will heal all ills, but a curse will follow him who takes it from the gypsies!'* "

•4• *The Gypsy Curse*

"WHAT a strange message!" exclaimed Nancy, repeating it.

"My daughter must have placed the note in the jewelled album before she died," Mrs Struthers explained, "although her reason for doing it puzzles me."

"It may be a good clue," declared Nancy. "Perhaps a member of her husband's tribe sent the note to her."

"Quite likely. I have always thought the writer meant it as a warning . . . perhaps to frighten my daughter."

"Yes," said Nancy. "Or even a friendly warning."

"What do you think the message meant?" Mrs Struthers asked.

Nancy shrugged. "Perhaps that the doll, which may light up or be adorned with shiny jewels, would bring bad luck to any owner but a gypsy."

"In that case, maybe you had better not search for it," said Mrs Struthers, alarmed. "I should not want any harm to come to you."

Nancy smiled. "Please don't worry. I'll be careful. The mystery is too intriguing to drop now."

"If you do find the doll, I'll see that you are properly compensated," the collector told her.

"My reward will be the fun I'll have searching for the doll," Nancy said quickly.

"And perhaps in adding to my collection for me," suggested Mrs Struthers.

"I think before I go," Nancy said, "I'd better see what dolls you have, so I shan't duplicate them."

During the next hour and a half Nancy made a thorough inspection of the figures in the cabinet. The task took longer than she had expected, for they were so fascinating she could not bring herself to pass over them lightly.

The variety of materials of which the dolls were made amazed the girl. Some were even fashioned from substances such as cornhusks and horsehair. One, an exquisitely carved figure moulded from a hard ink case, Mrs Struthers explained, was an ancient Chinese doll.

"It was used in China, not to play with, but for religious instruction to children," she said. "And this dear little lady," she added, picking up one in a quaint evening dress, "is Jenny Lind, the famous singer. You know, she first appeared in this country under the sponsorship of P. T. Barnum of circus fame."

"Oh, really?" Nancy exclaimed. "I see now that a person certainly can learn a lot about history by collecting dolls. What does the word 'doll' come from?"

"The origin of the word isn't quite clear, though many authorities believe it's a contraction of the English name Dorothy. But way back in old Saxon times there was a word 'dol', meaning figure, and even the Greeks used the word 'ei-DOL-on', which meant idol."

"One can even learn about a language from dolls," remarked Nancy, her eyes twinkling.

The girl's gaze roved to a French swordsman high in the cabinet. The stalwart fellow stood alertly on guard, with his tiny steel sabre poised as if about to duel with an imaginary opponent.

"How lovely!" exclaimed Nancy in delight.

As she removed the figure from its niche, something

sharp pierced her finger. The prick was deep and made Nancy wince.

"Why, the sword doll wounded me!" she laughed, rubbing her finger.

Mrs Struthers was amazed, for she had never noticed the sword was so sharp. Blood began to ooze from the girl's finger.

"I'll get you a bandage," the woman offered.

"Please don't bother. The prick is nothing."

Nancy wrapped a clean handkerchief round her finger and gingerly put the sword doll back on the shelf. Just then an outside door slammed. A moment later Rose came clumping angrily into the room.

"Home early, aren't you, dear?" her grandmother observed.

"Yes, and I'll never play with that horrid Charmaine again! She said I'm bossy and wild."

"Oh, Rose, why can't you behave like a little lady and get along with your playmates?" Mrs Struthers fretted.

" 'Cause I'm not a lady yet and anyway maybe I don't want to be one! Maybe I'll be . . . I might even be a gypsy!"

"Rose! Don't say that!" Mrs Struthers cried out.

Nancy, to relieve the tension, changed the subject by asking Rose again about the man and woman who had stolen the doll the previous day. Rose told her the man had dark eyes and hair, with a scar on his forehead. The woman, she said, had carrot-coloured hair.

Presently Nancy could not seem to hear Rose very well nor concentrate any longer upon what the girl was saying. Feeling weak and dizzy, she brushed a hand across her eyes. Everything in the room seemed blurred. As if from far away, she heard Rose cry in a shrill voice:

"Oh, look at Nancy, Granny! She's white as a ghost!"

"I feel . . . peculiar," mumbled Nancy.

Mrs Struthers grasped her arm, guiding her to a couch. Nancy collapsed upon it.

"What's the matter with her, Granny?" cried Rose, terror-stricken.

"I don't know. She was all right a moment ago. I can't understand . . ."

Nancy, fighting the dizziness, thought she knew what had caused her sudden illness. The girl realized that something must be done quickly.

"Send . . . for my . . . father," she pleaded, gasping for breath. "Tell him . . . to hurry!"

"Yes, yes!" murmured Mrs Struthers in a panic.

"A doctor . . ." whispered Nancy. "I think . . . the sword doll . . . poisoned . . . me!"

With that, she lapsed into unconsciousness.

• 5 • *Trouble at the Carnival*

AT Nancy's sudden collapse Mrs Struthers became hysterical. Her housekeeper, Mrs Carol, hurried into the room.

"Oh, Nancy's been poisoned!" Mrs Struthers wailed. "Call Mr Drew and Doctor Burney at once!"

The housekeeper, horrified, rushed to the telephone and summoned the two men, who reached the Struthers home at exactly the same moment. Mrs Struthers explained rather incoherently what had happened.

"There's the doll that pricked Nancy! She thought it poisoned her. Oh, this dreadful thing is all my fault!"

Doctor Burney hastily examined the girl. "She has been poisoned all right," he announced.

"Will she . . . is there . . ." Mr Drew could not bring

himself to finish the thought that his daughter's illness might prove fatal.

"Easy," advised the doctor. "The dose probably was a light one, and she'll be all right. I'd like to find out what it was, though, so I can give an antidote and hasten her recovery."

Mr Drew took the sword doll and cautiously examined it. It took him a few minutes before he found a tiny button at the hilt of the sword. When he pressed it, a needle shot out. From it dripped a single drop of fluid.

"Oh, how dreadful!" cried Mrs Struthers.

Doctor Burney, having identified the poison by its odour, prepared an antidote. "Your daughter probably will sleep heavily for an hour," he told the lawyer, "and should be kept quiet until tomorrow."

Mr Drew wanted to take Nancy home, but the doctor advised against this. Mrs Struthers assured the lawyer that Nancy would receive the best possible care at her home. He suggested that it might be helpful if Hannah Gruen came there to stay with Nancy for the night.

Mrs Struthers was agreeable to the plan, and twenty minutes later Mrs Gruen arrived in a taxi. She listened quietly to the doctor's orders, promising they would be carried out.

"Call me if Nancy fails to awaken within an hour," he instructed as he left the house.

When almost an hour had elapsed, and she had not wakened, Mr Drew began to grow alarmed all over again. As he was about to call the doctor, Nancy yawned and drowsily opened her eyes.

"Where am I?" she mumbled, sitting up.

"With Hannah and me," said her father, placing the girl back gently against the pillow. "Everything is all right."

Reassured, Nancy sighed and snuggled down for some more sleep. Mr Drew remained at her bedside for another hour. Then, satisfied that his daughter was out of danger, he left for a business conference which he had hastily postponed in order to come to the house.

The next morning, Mrs Struthers, who had slept little, came downstairs early. As she brought in her copy of the River Heights *Gazette* from the porch, her eyes caught a headline which made her gasp.

NANCY DREW POISONED
by MYSTERIOUS DOLL
at STRUTHERS' HOME

"Good gracious!" exclaimed the woman. "Where did they ever hear about this?"

She was sure that no one in the house had given the story to the newspaper. As her mind flew from one possibility to another, she stopped short in her thinking.

Rose!

Mrs Struthers recalled that her granddaughter had been away from the house after Nancy's accident the previous afternoon. Yes, it must have been Rose. As soon as Rose appeared, Mrs Struthers showed her the article and asked:

"Rose, what do you know about the paper getting this?"

"Nothing," the girl answered.

"Then how did the story get out? Didn't you tell anyone?"

"Only some kids down the street."

"And they told everyone else," said Mrs Struthers. "Oh, this is dreadful! The article even tells how that couple in the car stole our fan doll, and I didn't want any publicity about it. Whatever shall I do with you, Rose?"

The girl became sulky and would eat no breakfast. The situation was not relieved any when Nancy appeared and saw the newspaper account. She had completely recovered from the effects of the poison, but this new slant on the affair was both disturbing and embarrassing.

Excited friends, reading the article, soon began telephoning to inquire about her. Bess and George came in person, as well as Ned Nickerson, an Emerson College student who had long admired Nancy. He had driven over from a nearby boys' summer camp, where he was a counsellor, to see her. Discovering that Nancy was up and looking her usual self, he teased her about the publicity, then said:

"Hope you'll be well enough to go with me to the carnival in Claymore tomorrow night."

"I'll be there," laughed Nancy. "Why, my long sleep has given me lots of pep."

Ned came to the Drew home early the next evening, and they drove directly to Claymore. Nancy enjoyed the carnival with its gay crowds and many amusements. They stopped first at a shooting gallery, where Ned won a box of chocolates which he presented to Nancy.

"What shall we do next?" he asked. "Want to try the ferris wheel?"

Nancy shook her head. "Listen!" she exclaimed.

"To what? That gypsy's fiddle?"

"Are there gypsies in this carnival?"

"Sure, down at the far end. They have several fortune-telling tents. Want to have your future told?"

"Let's!"

"Not I," laughed Ned. "My future is pretty well set and I don't want any gypsy tampering with it. I'll go into business, prosper, and marry a certain golden-haired young lady named . . ."

"Come on, Ned," Nancy broke in. "I'm not so much interested in fortunes myself, but I do want to hear that violinist play. A case I'm interested in has something to do with a gypsy violinist."

They hastened to the tents, where a cluster of bright-eyed, bronze-skinned children stared at them. A woman in a dashing red and yellow skirt hurriedly took up her post in front of one of the fortune-telling tents. Her fierce, blazing eyes studied Nancy appraisingly.

"Cross my palm with silver and I will tell your fortune, pretty miss," she invited.

Nancy shook her head, for she was listening intently to a singing violin.

"Isn't that the *Hungarian Rhapsody*?" Nancy murmured to Ned. "Maybe the violonist is Romano!"

"Who's he?" demanded Ned with pretended suspicion of a rival. "A friend of yours?"

Nancy did not explain, for she noticed that the gypsy woman was listening attentively to every word she and Ned were saying. Her gaze was so penetrating that the girl felt ill at ease. Nevertheless, she asked the gypsy:

"May we speak to the violinist?"

"No, it is not allowed," the woman replied coldly.

Turning to a couple of children, she said something in the gypsies' Romany language which neither Ned nor Nancy could understand. One of the youngsters scurried away from the tent, and a moment later the violin playing ended abruptly.

"At least tell us the name of your gifted musician," Nancy urged the woman.

The gypsy shrugged her shoulders, then went into the tent.

"Nice, sociable people!" Ned commented.

Wandering on, he and Nancy tried to catch a glimpse of the violinist. Evidently warned by the child, he had fled inside a tent.

"Wonder why the gypsies are acting so strangely?" Ned remarked. "Maybe in asking to see him we violated some tribal rule."

"I think there's more to it than that," whispered Nancy. "See how everyone is watching us. We've aroused their suspicions about something."

As the couple walked along the row of tents, their every move seemed to be scrutinised by members of the gypsy tribe. No one again offered to tell Nancy's fortune. When a little boy came to Ned, whining for a coin, his mother spoke sharply in Romany from a nearby tent. The child scampered off without waiting for the coin Ned offered him.

"What's the matter with everybody?" he asked, puzzled.

"It's as if they're afraid we'll find out something they want to keep hidden!"

The longer Nancy and Ned stayed, the more tense the situation became, so finally they left and returned to the main section of the carnival. There they asked one of the concessionaires where the gypsies came from.

"Somewhere out west, I believe," the man replied. "Guess they're fixin' to leave the carnival a few days after the wedding."

"What wedding is that?" Nancy questioned.

"Why, the one tonight at nine o'clock. Didn't you see the sign? They're marrying off a child bride."

"No, we didn't see the sign," said Nancy. "I'd love to go to the ceremony! But I thought gypsy weddings were for gypsies only."

"They usually are," the man nodded. "This ône would have been, too, only the carnival manager got their chief, Zorus, to agree to let the public attend."

"For a fee, of course," smiled Ned.

"Oh, sure, a high one at that. But it's only tonight that outsiders can go. A gypsy wedding sometimes goes on for six or seven days with dancing and feasting."

"Where can we get tickets?" Ned asked.

"At the first gypsy tent from here. From what I'm told, it won't be worth the price, though. All that happens is that the chief speaks a few words, and they give the child bride a doll. Then the dancing begins. That's the best part."

Nancy's eyes kindled at the mention of a ceremony making use of a doll. She might pick up a clue! Then her eager expression turned to one of dismay.

"Ned," she said, "maybe the gypsies won't let us in!"

▪ 6 ▪ *The Child Bride*

NED AND NANCY purposely stayed away from the gypsy section of the carnival until nearly nine o'clock, hoping to be unobserved among the many people who might come to the wedding.

"If we go in separately, maybe they won't spot us," Nancy suggested.

She was right. Eager last-minute attendants at the performance jostled them and they were not noticed by the ticket seller or any other gypsies.

Music for the wedding was being furnished by three handsome young fiddlers. Nancy liked their gay, colourful costumes. Because of their age she knew none of them could be Rose's father. She listened as they played, then concluded that none of them had the fine touch of the violinist who had played the *Hungarian Rhapsody* so hauntingly a little while before.

"That other violinist could have been Romano Pepito," Nancy concluded. "Oh, how I wish I might see him!"

At this moment the musicians changed to another melody, soft and sweet. From a tent stepped a middle-aged man wearing a red and yellow suit and long, round earrings. He walked to the centre of the ring. Acting as master of ceremonies, he held up his hands, saying:

"According to gypsy custom, the price for the bride must be paid before the wedding takes place. In olden days horses were given, but now we gypsies prefer money."

The gaudily attired young bridegroom and the father of

the bride came forward. The former took a small pouch of jingling coins from a pocket and handed it to the other, who made a long speech in Romany. Then the three fiddlers struck up a solemn march.

"Oh, this must be the chief," thought Nancy, as a tall, elderly man in a long, embroidered red robe stalked from another tent. Piercing black eyes looked out above a heavy, iron-grey beard. He spoke to the other men, then the bride's father went into a tent.

"We are true gypsies," the master of ceremonies spoke up, "and our girls marry very young. But we have complied with all the laws of this state. Our leader Zorus will now unite Melchor and Luisa in a Romany wedding ceremony."

The musicians began playing a livelier air, but this did not help to calm the bride as she stepped nervously from her tent. Nancy's heart went out to the beautiful young girl, who looked very frightened and could not have been more than fourteen years old. She was dressed in an embroidered white silk gown which had become yellowed with age and frequent use.

The ceremony was performed by Zorus in the space of a few minutes. Nancy studied his face. It was cruel and calculating.

"I wouldn't trust him," thought Nancy.

A loaf of bread, salt, and a bottle of wine were brought out as symbols of plenty. Zorus broke the bread and sprinkled salt on each half. The bride and groom exchanged halves, each taking a bite and a sip of wine.

Zorus now motioned to the announcer, who said, "It has been a custom for hundreds of years, at weddings of our tribe, to present the child bride with a doll. Today our bride is not exactly a child, but nevertheless, we shall follow that custom."

Nancy watched intently as an elderly gypsy woman walked forward carrying a basket. Possibly Rose's father at the time of his marriage had given his bride a gypsy doll. It might have been a duplicate of the one about to be presented!

"If it was, and that's the one I'm to look for, I may be a long way towards solving Mrs Struthers' mystery," she thought excitedly.

When the gift was held up Nancy's hopes fell. It was only an inexpensive factory-made doll, and so new that it could have no significance for her.

In a few moments the violinists began to play for dancing, and the crowd milled around. Ned found Nancy and asked if she had enjoyed the ceremony.

"Oh, yes," she replied. "For just a second I thought I had found a good clue, but nothing came of it. Let's watch the performance a few minutes longer and then go home."

Though the tribal dances were interesting to watch, Nancy found her gaze wandering towards a middle-aged gypsy couple who stood off to one side.

"That man and woman look familiar to me," the girl thought. "And yet they're gypsies. I don't know any gypsies."

She noticed that they were staring at her, but when she faced them directly they hastily looked away and edged towards the exit.

"Why did they do that?" Nancy wondered.

Suddenly she believed she knew who they were. The man had a scar on his forehead. The woman had carrot-red hair. They fitted Rose's description of the couple who had stolen Mrs Struthers' fan doll!

Nancy motioned to Ned and guardedly hurried after them. Near a tent the suspects were stopped by an old gypsy woman who addressed the man as Anton and the woman as Nitaka.

"I think they might be the thieves who came to Mrs Struthers' in a black saloon!" Nancy whispered to Ned excitedly. "If so, their car must be parked on the grounds and there might be some evidence in it. Want to see if you can find it?"

"Sure thing. What's the licence number?"

"I don't know, Ned. But look for a black saloon of the same make and year as my car. I'll wait here for you. I want to watch Anton and Nitaka."

Ned slipped away quietly. Unnoticed, Nancy followed the gypsy couple. Presently they stopped and she sauntered up to them, asking a casual question about the wedding ceremony. Anton gazed at her with hostile eyes and made a brief reply.

Nancy then brought up the subject of dolls. Instead of talking to her, Anton said something to Nitaka in the Romany language. Rudely turning their backs, the couple walked away.

A few minutes later Nancy spied them talking earnestly and confidentially to old Zorus. As they left him, she caught a phrase of Nitaka's words to Anton, "—meddling girl." Did the woman mean her?

Ned returned to report that he had found not one but three black saloons which would answer Nancy's description. He also handed her a scrap of soiled paper.

"Found this on the ground near one of the cars," he explained. "It's a receipt that may interest you."

The paper read: "For one doll, $100—" The rest had been torn off and the names of both buyer and seller were missing.

"This certainly does interest me!" cried Nancy. "We must find the other part of the paper. Show me where you picked this up."

Ned led her to the dimly-lit car park. "The note was lying on the ground by this black car," he pointed out. "There was no other paper anywhere around."

"This car looks like the one that stopped at the Struthers'," Nancy said. "Maybe if we wait, we'll see who the owner is. And if he should turn out to be Anton or Nitaka . . ."

"Hey, not so fast," laughed Ned.

He and Nancy searched the ground for the missing part of the receipt but did not find it. Presently they heard someone coming.

"It may be Anton or Nitaka!" whispered Nancy tensely.

Slipping behind another parked car, they saw a young man walk over rapidly to the car and unlock the door. Ned came out of hiding.

"Just a minute, sir!" he said. "May we ask you a few questions?"

Startled, the fellow whirled round. Then Ned burst into laughter.

"Bill Jones!" he exclaimed, recognising a college friend whom Nancy also knew.

"From the way you spoke, I take it you thought I was a crook!" Bill grinned after he had greeted Nancy and her escort.

"Something like that," Ned admitted. "Is this your car?"

"It will be when I finish the payments on it. What are you and Nancy doing here? Sleuthing?"

"We came to see the carnival," Nancy explained, "but now we're looking for some thieves."

"Sorry I can't oblige you," Bill teased. "Want a lift to River Heights?"

"No, thanks, Bill, we have a car," Ned replied.

Nancy and Ned waited until the owners of the other black saloons came along, but they were not Anton, Nitaka, or any other gypsies.

"Well, I certainly failed on all my clues tonight," said Nancy as they walked to their own car. "Or did I? Maybe learning who those suspects are will be worthwhile."

Nancy's exciting visit to the carnival did not prevent her from sleeping soundly. After awakening the next morning, she lay in bed for a few minutes to recall the evening's events.

"Yes?" she said, hearing Hannah Gruen call her name from the hall.

George Fayne was on the telephone, reminding Nancy of the yacht club meeting for older girls that morning. "You're going to go this time, and Bess and I just won't take 'No' for an answer," she said with pretended sternness.

Nancy laughed. "What happened at the last meeting?"

"Oh, didn't I tell you? It was postponed."

"I'll be over in an hour," Nancy promised.

She picked up Bess and George in her car and they arrived at the club to find a chattering crowd of girls, all speculating on what the president's announcement was to be. Presently he rapped for order.

"Young ladies," he said, a twinkle in his eye, "it has been voted to invite you to enter the Dixon cup races this year."

"Oh, wonderful!" cried the athletic George and several other girls.

"Just what you were hoping for, Nancy," said Bess.

"But where will we get a boat?" demanded George.

"There's to be an auction of used boats at Jefferson next Monday," he said. "Several sailing dinghies are among them. One's a beauty . . . said to be faster than anything in River Heights," he smiled. "She's called the *Lass*."

"I'll be in Jefferson bright and early on Monday," sang out a girl named Phyllis Bean.

When the meeting broke up, George suggested that she, Nancy and Bess buy the *Lass* and sail her in the race.

"Oh, we could never win," said Bess, who was not particularly athletic-minded. "Why bother?"

"And I can't neglect my mystery," Nancy added teasingly. Then she said with a twinkle in her eye, "It just so happens that I'm going over to Jefferson on Monday."

"Really?" cried George.

"To attend a sale of dolls for Mrs Struthers," Nancy explained.

"Then why don't we drive over together and look at the *Lass*?" exclaimed George enthusiastically.

"I'd planned to go by plane," said Nancy.

"All the better," declared George. "I hope our parents will let us buy a boat."

She and Bess obtained consent from their parents within an hour. Nancy had to wait until dinnertime that evening to broach the subject.

"I'd be glad to have you share in the ownership of a good sailing dinghy," Carson Drew assured his daughter. "If the craft looks all right and the bidding doesn't go too high, buy it. I'll trust your judgement."

"Dad, have you a date tonight?" Nancy asked when they had finished dinner. "Or will you go somewhere with me?"

"With *you*?" he replied, chuckling and making a half-bow. "I'd be delighted."

"Maybe you won't be so delighted when you hear what it is. I'd like to take Rose to the carnival . . ."

"Oh, no!"

"Only to have her look at Anton and Nitaka to see if they're the ones who stole the fan doll."

"That's different," said Mr Drew. "All right."

Mrs Struthers consented to the plan, and Rose was thrilled. But to Nancy's disappointment the manager told them the tribe had moved out early that morning.

"That old fellow Zorus was a strange guy," he said. "Never even said they were leaving."

"How about Anton and Nitaka?" Nancy asked. "Did they go with the others?"

"I didn't know any of 'em except their king."

"King?" said Mr Drew. "Was Zorus their king?"

"That's what they called him," the manager explained. "And treated him like one, too."

Nancy reflected on this bit of information as she and her father drove home. Were the two she suspected of stealing Mrs Struthers's doll subjects of Zorus? Had he perhaps instructed them to take it?

"Guess you scared them away," Mr Drew broke in on his daughter's thoughts.

"I'll keep on looking for that couple just the same," Nancy said with a grim smile.

"That spirit should win anything for you," her father teased. "Even the dinghy race."

"If I find a sailing dinghy," Nancy laughed.

At nine o'clock on Monday morning, Bess and George met Nancy at the River Heights airport.

"Oh, Nancy," George said, "I just heard Phyl Bean and her crowd left yesterday by car for Jefferson. I'm so afraid they'll buy the *Lass* before we can get there."

"It's an auction and doesn't start till ten. We'll make it," Nancy assured her.

George continued to worry, but Nancy scarcely heard what she said. Her attention suddenly focused on a woman who at that moment was entering the waiting plane.

The passenger was Nitaka!

·7·   "Whip the Wind"

NANCY nudged Bess and George. "Nitaka just got on the plane!" she whispered excitedly.

"You mean that carrot-haired woman?" Bess asked. "She isn't wearing gypsy clothes."

"The woman who stole Mrs Struthers' doll wasn't

wearing them at the time, either," said Nancy. "The gypsies left the carnival, but evidently they didn't go far away," she guessed.

"Where do you suppose Nitaka's going?" George asked.

"I have no idea, but I mean to follow her, now that I have a chance," Nancy decided quickly. "If she doesn't get off at Jefferson, I'll stay on the plane until she does."

"Oh, please don't," said Bess. "You might get into trouble!"

"What about the boat?" George cried in dismay. "And the doll sale?"

"You girls will have to go to them." As the cousins groaned and insisted they could not do the jobs without her, Nancy added, "If Nitaka *is* a thief and she should lead me to something important, you wouldn't want me to give up the chase, would you?"

"Oh, I suppose not," George said grudgingly.

A moment before the take-off the three girls went aboard and seated themselves at the rear of the plane. Not once during the flight to Jefferson did the gypsy woman glance over her shoulder. She seemed indifferent to the scenery, devoting herself to a booklet which she read many times.

The girls were the first passengers off the plane when it landed at Jefferson. They kept out of sight and watched to see whether the gypsy would alight also. Nancy had just about decided she was not going to, when Nitaka appeared. The woman hastened through the waiting-room and jumped into a cab.

"Hurry, or we'll lose her!" Nancy cried to her friends, who had lingered to watch a plane take off.

After a little delay they found another taxi. By this time Nitaka's cab was far down the road.

"Will you please try to overtake that taxi?" Nancy asked their driver.

The elderly man was none too willing, and as they

reached the heart of Jefferson, it became evident they had completely lost the trail of the other vehicle.

"It turned down a side street somewheres," their driver mumbled. "I was watchin' sharp, but I didn't see which way it went."

"Never mind," sighed Nancy.

Secretly George was rather glad the chase had ended, for she was eager to go on to the boat basin.

"Let's drive there right away," she pleaded, looking at her watch which read nine-fifty.

"We still have ten minutes," Nancy encouraged her.

She asked the driver to go at once to Pier 45. It took fifteen minutes and they found the auction already in progress. A group of perhaps thirty persons was there to bid on used boats of various sizes and models which were tied up along the quay. The *Lass* had not been put up yet.

"There's Phyl over there!" exclaimed George. "The Drake twins are with her. They're all swell sailors."

"Don't be so fidgety," Bess scolded her cousin. "What if we don't get the boat?"

"Phyl is out to win the race," George declared.

"And so are you," Bess teased.

The three girls sauntered over to look at the *Lass*, which Phyllis also was inspecting.

"I'm prepared to outbid anyone who tries to buy this!" she remarked significantly.

"She's a neat little craft," Nancy observed, but whispered to George that she did not especially like the look of the mast.

Presently the *Lass* was put up for sale. Two hundred dollars was the opening bid. Nancy raised it by fifty. The man jumped ten. When Nancy reluctantly bid another five, he remained silent.

"Two hundred and seventy!" Phyllis called clearly.

"Seventy-five!" cried Nancy, then whispered to George and Bess, "Keep bidding, and stall the auctioneer as long as you can. But try not to go over three hundred dollars."

"Where are you going?" asked Bess as Nancy started away.

"I'll be right back."

Leaving her friends to wonder what possessed her, Nancy moved hurriedly down the dock. She had noticed that a number of weather-beaten boats which had not been among those in the auction were being moved into position and made fast along the wharf. She asked if they were to be included in the sale.

"That's right, miss," a dock hand replied. "Lookin' fer a fast racin' boat?"

"Yes, I am."

"Then here's your baby." The man pointed to a trim craft which looked a little shabby but only for want of paint. "She's the *Whip the Wind*—won six races straight last summer."

"Then why is she being sold?"

"The owner took sick and is givin' up sailin'. Didn't even have a chance to paint her for the sale today. But she's the best boat here."

"She's beautiful—simply beautiful," Nancy said admiringly, her eyes taking in the craft's fine lines. "But I can't afford to pay very much——"

"She may go cheap," the man predicted with a grin. "Most of the folks with money in their pockets who came here today have already picked out their boats. They didn't know *Whip the Wind* was going to be put up."

Highly elated, Nancy ran back to her friends. George had just been outbid on the *Lass* by five dollars and was frantic the boat would be knocked down to their rival Phyllis.

"The bidding has already gone to three hundred and five," she wailed.

"Let her go."

"But, Nancy——"

"Better boats will come along."

"Oh, Nancy!" With a groan of anguish, George heard the auctioneer award the *Lass* to Phyllis for three hundred and twenty-five dollars.

"Don't take it so hard," Nancy consoled her. "Just be patient."

Several other boats were auctioned off, each bringing a good price.

"The best ones are gone," George complained. "No use buying an old tub. We may as well go."

Nancy smiled and refused to budge. Finally the auctioneer directed the attention of the crowd to *Whip the Wind.* Bidding began again.

"There's our boat!" whispered Nancy.

Without appearing too eager, she entered a low bid. It was topped. Nancy then offered a hundred and seventy-five dollars. This was bettered and she called "Two hundred." There were no other bids.

"Sold to the little lady in the blue dress," the man announced.

"I hope you know what you're doing," George said nervously to Nancy. "Will she race?"

"All she needs is a little paint to make her the trimmest craft in her class in River Heights," Nancy defended her purchase, and told of *Whip the Wind*'s record.

"Gosh, you're wonderful, Nancy!" George promptly slapped her friend on the back.

After inspecting the craft, Nancy was more than ever convinced they had made an excellent buy. *Whip the Wind*'s sails and rigging were in perfect condition and her seams were tight.

"The wind should be just right to sail back to River Heights this afternoon," she announced with enthusiasm. "It's a long trip, but with a spanking breeze off our stern we could make good time."

"It should give us some practice for the race, too," agreed George. "Let's do it!"

Bess was none too keen about the trip, but her objections were promptly overruled. While Nancy was paying for the boat, Phyllis, looking somewhat grim, came over to inspect it.

"Think you'll get that old tub to River Heights without her falling apart?" she laughed.

"Want to race?" challenged George.

"No, thanks!" Phyllis retorted, turning away. "I'm having my new boat taken home by road."

Nancy had spent more time at the auction than she had intended. Now it was after eleven and she feared many of the dolls at the Jefferson Galleries might have been sold.

"We'll have to hurry or we'll be too·late," she declared, and summoned a cab. "I hope I haven't failed Mrs Struthers."

Ten minutes later the girls were at the Jefferson Galleries. The salerooms were thronged with customers. Nancy was relieved to learn that while nearly all the fine old silver and jewellery had been sold, not many of the dolls had been.

"Why did Mrs Struthers want you to come to this particular sale?" Bess asked as the girls walked towards the counter where the dolls were displayed.

"Most of the dolls are old and valuable, so there's a chance the stolen fan doll is here, and even the one Mrs Struthers' daughter wanted her to find," Nancy explained.

She examined them all carefully. Finding none which she wanted, she asked a salesman if he had any others for sale which were not on display—any which lit up or had gems sewn on their costumes.

"The most attractive dolls have been sold," he answered. "One like you mention was among them. A king with a jewelled robe."

"Just my luck!" groaned Nancy. Then, thinking perhaps

she might get it from the purchaser, she asked, "Who bought the doll?"

"The woman didn't give her name. She paid cash. Oh, there she is now—leaving with her package."

Turning quickly, Nancy caught a glimpse of the retreating figure who was now outside the galleries. Nitaka!

Nancy ran after the gypsy, but was too late to stop her. Nitaka entered a taxi and already was far down the street before the girl reached the pavement.

"This is the worst yet!" she said, returning to Bess and George. "That woman may have bought the very doll I'm trying to find!"

The manager overheard Nancy's remark. Introducing himself, he said:

"If you're interested in fine dolls, perhaps you'd like to see one that is more valuable than any sold here today."

"Is it for sale?" Nancy asked, hope reviving in her.

"No, and we have never displayed the doll. Wait here and I'll bring it from the back room."

The manager was gone at least ten minutes. When he returned, the waiting girls saw at once that something was wrong.

"What became of that doll we kept in the office safe?" he asked several salesmen.

"You removed it this morning," one of the men reminded him.

"Yes, one of the doll's hands needed repairing. I took it out of the safe and put it on my desk. Now it's gone! Someone must have sold it by mistake!"

Each of the salesmen denied any part in such a transaction.

"Then the doll has been stolen!" the manager cried. "In the hands of the wrong person, it can be a very dangerous thing!"

· 8 · The Pick-pocket

NANCY asked the manager of the Jefferson Galleries what he meant about the doll being dangerous, but he was reluctant to reveal why.

"Is it because the doll is one of the poison type?" she asked.

The man gave her a startled glance. "Why . . . er . . . yes, it is," he admitted nervously. "We intended to sell the witch doll to a museum, and therefore hadn't removed the poisonous powder from it. When you touch a certain spot the powder sifts out. Its fumes induce deep sleep. An overdose could be fatal!"

"Oh!" cried Bess.

"You'll notify the police and the newspapers at once?" suggested Nancy. "If the information is published, the thief will be warned before he's harmed."

"Yes, I'll call them right now," the manager promised, starting away, but mumbled something about how it would serve the thief right if he was poisoned.

The girls were about to leave the galleries when Nancy spied a half-opened chest filled with dolls. A salesman came towards her, asking if she were interested.

"There are some unusual items in this chest," he said. "Here's one that may interest you," he added, offering Nancy a strange-looking figure with four different faces. "It dates back to about 1870."

One side of the porcelain head laughed, one cried, another pouted, and the fourth had its eyes closed as if in sleep.

49

The head rotated in a socket so that a child playing with the doll could choose whatever expression she desired.

"How much is this one?" Nancy asked. She felt sure Mrs Struthers would like to add it to her collection.

The man mentioned a price far below what she had expected, so she quickly made the purchase. While he went to wrap it, Nancy inspected the other dolls, but found nothing of special interest.

"Let's go," George urged as soon as the salesman came back. "If we're sailing to River Heights, we should start soon."

"Just a minute."

Nancy's gaze had fastened upon a counter stacked with albums. Eagerly she began looking among the old plush-covered books. Several were family albums decorated with raised, ornate wordings.

"Albums like those aren't unusual," George said impatiently. "My grandmother has a couple of them. Please come!"

But Nancy went on looking through the stack of albums. Then a name on one at the bottom of the pile caught her eye:

Euphemia Struthers.

Eagerly Nancy flipped the pages, but was disappointed to find that every photograph had been removed. Nevertheless, hopeful that this Euphemia might have been related to Mrs Struthers, and that the album by some chance contained the clue at which Rose's mother had hinted on her death-bed, Nancy purchased the book.

"Now let's leave before you find something else to buy!" George pleaded, pulling Nancy away.

The girls lunched at a tearoom across the street, and ordered sandwiches to take with them aboard *Whip the Wind*. Nancy sent a telegram to her father, telling him of their plan to sail the boat to River Heights.

"Dad will call your folks, so they'll know where you are

if we're becalmed for a week," Nancy said, her eyes twinkling.

"Becalmed for a week!" Bess exclaimed. "And me with a special date for Thursday!"

"I was joking," laughed Nancy. "We're more likely to run into storms."

"A storm would be worse than being becalmed! Oh, dear, must we sail the boat? Why not have it transported as Phyllis is doing with hers?"

"Oh, don't be silly!" George scoffed. "Who's afraid of a little wind? We're supposed to be sailors."

"Fair-weather ones," Bess insisted. "In rough weather, I know I'd get sick."

Nancy and George were convinced that no matter what the weather was, the trip would give them good experience for the race.

Bess held up her hands resignedly. "All right, you win. I'll go."

With the help of an old sailor, they checked *Whip the Wind* from stem to stern, satisfying themselves everything was shipshape.

Since the afternoon promised to be a hot one, the girls packed away several bottles of cold drinks in the storage box. Then they cast off, sailing with a brisk wind down the Forked River.

"If this breeze holds, we'll make wonderful time all the way home," Nancy declared, settling herself at the tiller. "Look at the old girl shift!"

From the stern of *Whip the Wind* a long trail of froth and foam indicated the craft was making good time. For several miles she sailed before the wind. Then the breeze showed signs of shifting.

"This *would* happen to us," George grumbled. "If we have to start tacking before we reach the bay, it means a long, hard pull."

As Nancy hauled in the sail a notch, she noticed a motorboat approaching from the distant shore. The speeding craft made a heavy swell.

When the boat came closer, the girls read the name *Top Rail* on the side. Only one man was in it, and from his attire, a business suit, they knew he was not on a fishing jaunt.

"Haven't we seen him somewhere?" Nancy remarked, as the *Top Rail* passed scarcely a dozen yards from the sailing dinghy. As the pilot glanced up from the wheel, gazing directly at Nancy, she exclaimed, "Why, it's the pick-pocket! The man who stole Mrs Struthers' bag at the recital!"

Nancy had raised her voice, forgetting how far sound carries across water. The man in the motor-boat apparently heard her. With a wide sweep of the wheel, he turned his craft sharply, heading towards shore.

"He knows we recognised him!" Nancy exclaimed. "He's running away!"

"Look out!" cried George, ducking to avoid the boom, which suddenly swung round. "The wind has changed! We're jibbing!"

The sail was flapping wildly, threatening to tear the rigging apart. Forgetting the motorboat for an instant, Nancy brought their own craft back into the wind.

"That was a close call," Bess gasped, as the boat steadied and got under way. "Please don't do that again!"

"I was so amazed at seeing the pick-pocket, I forgot to keep an eye on our sail. Bess, did you see where he went?"

"He's turning into an inlet!"

"We'll never overtake him," George spoke up, as Nancy headed after him. "Are you sure he was the pick-pocket?"

"I'm certain!"

"We can't catch him at this speed," said Bess. "Let's give it up!"

Nancy could not bring herself to go past the inlet without making an attempt to catch the thief. Reaching it, she sailed the craft only a short distance upstream, for the motorboat was nowhere in sight.

Realising it was a hopeless chase, Nancy pulled in to a nearby timber-yard pier. Going ashore, she asked several persons if they had seen the *Top Rail* pass that way. No one had noticed it.

"The boat seems to have vanished," she reported to the girls. "We may as well go home."

At least an hour had been lost. To delay them further, the wind was rapidly falling off.

"We'll soon be in a dead calm if this keeps up," George observed as they came about and headed for the river again.

Nancy, scanning the clouds, shook her head. "I'd say we're in for a storm. It probably won't break for some time, though."

The prospect of being drenched was not a cheering one. Pressing on down the Forked River, Nancy strove to make *Whip the Wind* sail faster.

At the entrance to the bay she carefully studied the course. By cutting directly across the bay at least ten miles could be saved. But would the storm hold off?

"Let's take the quickest way," George urged as Nancy hesitated.

"It would be safer to hug the shore," argued Bess nervously. "The storm may catch us out in the bay."

"Oh, I don't believe it'll amount to much," George replied. "If this breeze holds, we ought to reach the other side in less than an hour. Think of all the time we'll save."

"All right," Bess agreed. "I hope we're not making a mistake."

For half an hour the boat sailed well under Nancy's and George's skilful hands. But the sky steadily darkened, giving the water a black, ominous cast.

"I wish we'd taken the inner route," Bess remarked. "Can't we turn back?"

"Too late now," said Nancy, shortening sail, as the wind started ripping into them.

"It's too far to swim if anything goes wrong," wailed Bess, almost in tears. "We'd never make it!"

Nancy, grimly trying to keep the small craft steady on her course, anxiously watched the black clouds which were rapidly gathering overhead.

"Better see that everything's secure, girls," she said. "It's going to pour any minute. Try and find room in the storage box for my packages, will you?"

Without warning a squall struck the boat from the stern with such terrific force that it carried the boom far out over the water. *Whip the Wind* yawed wildly.

"We're going to capsize!" screamed Bess.

"Bess! George! Shift your weight to starboard!" ordered Nancy, frantically grabbing at the sheet. "And hang on for your lives!"

• 9 •   *Bad News*

As THE boat heeled over, Nancy strained every muscle to keep the sail from coming down on the water. If that should happen, *Whip the Wind* would indeed capsize.

"Oh!" shrieked Bess. "This is terrible! We'll be drowned!"

George, more courageous than her cousin, applied herself to assisting Nancy. One more terrific gust knocked the breath from the girls! Nancy nearly lost control of the craft. For a few moments it was touch and go, and it was only by the most skilful handling that she and George kept the boat from going over.

"I can't stand much more of this!" Bess wailed.

"Oh, be quiet!" George shouted above the roar of the wind.

"The gale—is beginning—to die down," Nancy encouraged the girl breathlessly.

In a few minutes the wind stopped blowing so hard and the craft nosed through the water more smoothly.

"Oh, Nancy, we're safe!" breathed Bess, her eyes filled with tears of joy and relief.

"I thought for a while our number was up!" said George.

"So did I!" Nancy replied. "The——"

Another furious gust of wind hit them. Nancy braced herself, straining to hold the sheet. The rope cut deep ridges in her hands, but she held on and two minutes later won the battle.

"Please, let's take the inside route the rest of the way," Bess pleaded. "It'll be safer even if it is longer."

"All right," Nancy consented, heading for an inlet. "It's anyone's guess when we'll reach River Heights, though!"

The wind slackened, but the rain began to fall in torrents, until the girls were unable to see twenty feet in front of them.

"We'll be lucky if we can get in without hitting something," said George, worried.

"If you see a light or anything, shout," Nancy directed. "There may be other boats in the bay!"

Bess watched carefully. Fortunately they met no other craft, and in ten minutes the storm passed.

"Now we can dry ourselves!" Bess called. "But I'll never look the same!"

"Look, there's a rainbow!" exclaimed Nancy. "That's supposed to bring good luck."

"At least I hope our bad luck has gone!" said George.

The inside route over three connecting rivers was slow and tedious. Frequently trees blanketed the breeze, slowing the boat almost to a crawl. When this happened, the girls took turns at the oars. Dusk found the voyagers still many miles from their destination.

"We can't keep on after dark without danger of running aground," Nancy spoke up. "There'll not be a moon tonight. We'll have to stop."

"I couldn't sail another mile anyway, I'm so tired," Bess said. "But where can we stop?"

"We might stay at a farmhouse," George proposed.

"How about a tourist camp?" Nancy suggested. "I think I see one along the shore."

She pointed towards a group of log cabins visible on a green slope ahead. Sailing closer, soon the girls were near enough to read a sign advertising cabins at ten dollars a night. Tying up at the jetty, they arranged for lodging and supper. Then, after telephoning home, they went to bed.

"Don't anyone wake me before nine," Bess ordered.

Completely worn out, she slept long after the others the next morning. When she awakened, sunlight was streaming in the windows.

"No more storms," she thought happily. Then, noticing that the adjoining bunks were empty, she jumped out of bed. "It must be late!" she told herself.

Getting into her clothes hurriedly, Bess dashed outside. She could not see Nancy or George anywhere. *Whip the Wind* was still tied up at the jetty.

"At least they didn't go off in it and leave me," she grinned.

Bess wandered about but the other girls did not show up. Feeling slighted, she breakfasted alone and returned to the cabin. George had just arrived.

"Where have you been, and where's Nancy?" Bess asked in a hurt tone.

"I don't know where Nancy went. Sleuthing, I suppose. Been doing a little of it myself," said George. "Would Lazy Bones like to hear what I did?"

Bess ignored the thrust. "Is it worth hearing?" she countered.

"It sure is. I found out at the post office that the pick-pocket stole that boat *Top Rail*."

"Really?" cried Bess, interested at once. "Did he bring it back?"

"He abandoned the boat in some bushes, but I'll bet the old crook would have disguised it and sold it, if he hadn't seen Nancy," George said. "Oh, here comes Nancy now. She looks excited!"

The girl's eyes were bright from the early morning walk and she was a little short of breath from hurrying.

"Girls, see what I found!" she cried, holding up a soiled and badly stained piece of paper.

"Looks like an old concert programme," said George.

"That's exactly what it is! And see whose name is featured—Romano Pepito's!"

"The gypsy violinist!" exclaimed George. "Where did you find it?"

"In a field not far from here."

Nancy related that soon after starting her walk she had come to a deserted camp site by the river. Looking around, she deduced from bits of evidence here and there that a gypsy caravan had pulled away from the spot not many hours before.

"A tattered old tent was left behind," Nancy continued. "It was in there that I found the programme."

"Then someone in the caravan may have known Romano Pepito," Bess commented.

"He may even have been with them himself!" Nancy declared. "Oh, I'd give anything to follow that gypsy caravan and find out if Romano Pepito is in it."

"Remember, we have a boat that must be sailed to River Heights," George reminded her.

"True enough," Nancy agreed, "but there's no hurry.

Suppose I phone home and find out how everything is; then we can decide what to do."

While Bess and George waited, Nancy went to the main cabin to telephone Hannah Gruen. Five minutes later she returned.

"I have to change all my plans," she said anxiously. "I can't follow the gypsies and I can't sail with you!"

"What?" they demanded together.

"Hannah thinks I should take a train and come home right away."

"Why, what's wrong?" Bess inquired.

"Something happened at Mrs Struthers's home. Hannah didn't know just what it was, because Mrs Carol wouldn't say. Rose is sick in bed owing to it and her grandmother too. They've been asking for me."

"I suppose you'll have to go," sighed Bess.

"I'm terribly sorry to leave you two alone with the boat, but you won't mind, will you?" Nancy smiled.

"As long as we stay off that bay!" said Bess.

George was disappointed, but tried not to let Nancy know how she felt.

"We'll do our best," she said. "It may take us an age to reach River Heights, though, because we're not as good sailors as you, Nancy."

"You're wrong there," Nancy assured her. "You're grand sailors."

Waving goodbye, Bess and George cast off, while Nancy arranged with the tourist-cabin owner to drive her to the nearest railway station. Fortunately she was able to get a train in thirty minutes, and within an hour and a half arrived in River Heights. She taxied directly to the Struthers' home, and was admitted by the housekeeper.

"I'm so glad you've come," Mrs Carol said. "Matters are in a bad state here."

"What's wrong?"

"A child in the neighbourhood, Janie Bond, started a

story that Rose's father was a gypsy. To make it worse, she said all gypsies are thieves!"

"Oh, how dreadful!" cried Nancy. "Rose's father was a talented violinist."

"Yes, I know," said the housekeeper. "Mrs Struthers told me the whole story this morning, but she hasn't told Rose a thing."

"Oh, and why not?"

"I don't know, and naturally Rose believes what Janie says. Won't you see what you can do with Mrs Struthers?"

"Is she still in bed?"

"Yes, and getting more beside herself by the minute. I wanted to call the doctor, but she wouldn't let me."

Nancy hurried up the stairs and went directly to Mrs Struthers.

"Oh, Nancy, what am I going to do?" the anxious woman wailed.

Nancy took Mrs Struthers' hand in her own and tried to calm her. "Please don't be so upset," she said. "Children say things without thinking and forget them the next minute."

"But not this," Mrs Struthers said, trembling. "The disgrace of it! Things were bad enough before, but now to have everyone think my daughter married a thief!"

"Please, Mrs Struthers. Intelligent people know most gypsies are fine people, and wouldn't believe little Janie Bond."

Nancy went on to say that what other people thought was of far less importance anyway than what the blow might do to Rose.

"She's a sensitive girl and if things aren't straightened out in her mind she may do something drastic."

"In what way?" asked Mrs Struthers, startled.

"Oh, run away, for instance."

The woman looked at Nancy with frightened eyes. She did not speak for several seconds, then said, "Nancy, you are a very wise person. I can see I lost my head completely. I'll tell Rose everything at once!"

As the woman got out of bed Nancy laid a restraining hand on her shoulder. "Would you like to suggest to Rose that on account of his work her father was unable to come back to his family at the time, but that he will as soon as he can?"

Mrs Struthers smiled. "It is very good advice. I'll take it. Will you come with me?"

"No, I'll wait downstairs."

Mrs Struthers went to Rose's room and stayed for half an hour. Then the two of them came downstairs.

How changed both were! They were actually smiling at each other! Nancy learned that the only barrier not crossed was that Rose stubbornly refused to return to school, fearing the other children might make fun of her.

Again Mrs Struthers appealed to Nancy, who thought a moment, then said, "Why don't you arrange to have Rose tutored at home and add music and dancing to her studies?"

"Oh, please let me, Granny!" cried the girl. "And I want to play the violin like my father!"

"All right," Mrs Struthers agreed. "Whom do you recommend, Nancy? I don't know any teachers in River Heights."

Nancy knew an excellent retired schoolteacher and gave Mrs Struthers her address, as well as those of the best music and dancing teachers in River Heights. Mrs Struthers thanked her profusely for her help.

"I must talk to Janie Bond," Nancy decided as she left the house. "How in the world did that girl learn Rose is part gypsy?"

At the school Nancy found out from some little girls who Janie was and stopped her as she started home. The child became frightened when she realised she was to be questioned about Rose.

"I don't know anything about her," she said sullenly. "So let me go home."

"Who told you Rose is a gypsy?"

"I'm not going to tell!"

"Then I'll ask your mother." Nancy walked off in the direction of the Bond home.

"No, wait!" Frantically Janie ran after her. "Don't tell Mum about the story I started!" she pleaded. "I'll tell you the truth about anything you want to know!"

·10· *The Rescue*

"THAT's better," said Nancy, halting. "Who told you Rose is a gypsy?"

"A strange woman," Janie explained. "I was in front of our school one day with some kids when she drove up. She asked us if Rose had come out yet."

"And you said?"

"That Rose had gone home."

"Did the woman look like a gypsy?"

Janie shrugged. "She was real dark and had red hair and wore big earrings. She asked us a lot of questions about Rose."

"What were they?"

"She wanted to know what time Rose came to school and what time she went home—oh, everything about her. Then she told us Rose's father was a gypsy. That's all."

"But that's not all of the story you told to the other children."

"I made up the rest," Janie admitted. "I'm sorry. Honestly I am."

"Rose is the daughter of a great violinist," Nancy told the girl. "I've heard, too, that he's a gypsy, but that's nothing to his discredit. Most gypsies are fine people. Some are excellent musicians and a few of them are film stars."

Feeling ashamed, Janie tried to slip away. Nancy, however, was not ready to let her go until she had learned more about the mysterious woman who had spoken of Rose's being a gypsy.

"Did the lady drive up in a black saloon?" she asked.

"Yes, and she got real mad when Billy West upset her suitcase."

"Suitcase?"

"She had a little one in her hand when she got out of the car. Billy pushed against it and it opened up. Guess what she had inside!"

"You tell me."

"Dolls! I guess she must sell them, only they didn't look new. The kids all wanted to see them, but the woman was real cross about it. She closed the suitcase with a bang."

"Did you see the dolls yourself, Janie?"

"Sure, I was standing right there all the time."

"What were they like?" Nancy asked excitedly.

"Oh, they weren't like the ones in the shops. One had a fan in her hand. Another was a little man playing a violin."

Janie's carelessly given information convinced Nancy that the woman was none other than the one who had stolen Mrs Struthers' fan doll. The description Janie had given fitted Nitaka.

"Did the doll with the fan stand on a little velvet box?" Nancy inquired eagerly.

"I think so," Janie recalled. "The woman slammed the suitcase shut so fast we didn't get a very good look at the dolls. Billy asked her if she sold them. She said yes. Then she jumped in her car and drove away."

Nancy's suspicions were confirmed. Not only was she certain that the woman with the dolls was Nitaka, but that a plot was afoot to harm Rose.

"May I go now?" Janie asked impatiently. "I promise I won't make up any more stories about Rose."

"All right, Janie," Nancy said. "But if you ever see the woman with the dolls again, please let me know right away." She wrote her name and address on a slip of paper.

Nancy was tempted to reveal to Mrs Struthers what she had learned, then thought better of it. The woman already was in a highly nervous state, and the information that Rose might be in danger would only upset her more. Nancy sought her father's advice on what to do. He shared her alarm about Rose's safety and said at once that a detective should be assigned to the Struthers' grounds.

"We can't do that without telling Mrs Struthers," Nancy replied, "and I don't want to worry her."

"Tell you what," Mr Drew decided. "I'll engage the detective on my own responsibility and tell him not to let the Struthers know he is on duty. After this has blown over, if Mrs Struthers feels the service has been worth while she can pay me for it."

Mr Drew telephoned a detective he knew, and explained what he was to do. The lawyer had just hung up when the telephone rang. He answered, then handed the receiver to his daughter.

"It's for you, Nancy. Mrs Marvin."

In an agitated voice Bess's mother said that her daughter and George had not reached River Heights yet in *Whip the Wind*, and no message had been received from them. "I'm dreadfully worried," she added, "and Mrs Fayne is too."

Taking a quick glance out of the window, Nancy noticed that not a leaf was stirring.

"I imagine the boat has been becalmed somewhere along the way," she reassured Mrs Marvin. "Suppose I go after them with a motorboat?"

"If you only would!" Mrs Marvin exclaimed, deeply grateful.

Without wasting a minute, Nancy drove to the dock and from there got in touch with a friend of her father's who owned a fast motorboat. Thirty minutes later they sighted *Whip the Wind.*

"Oh, Nancy," Bess said when the motorboat came alongside, "you're like a gift from heaven! We're scorched to a cinder. Get us off this miserable old tub, and take us home!"

"After you left we had a terrible time," George added. "The wind kept dropping, so I couldn't get any speed out of the boat to offset the tide. I'm afraid she isn't as fast as you thought, Nancy."

"No boat will sail without wind," declared Nancy tactfully. "Want to be towed in?"

"Naturally," said Bess, stepping stiffly into the motorboat. "I've had enough of this."

Nancy wet a finger and held it up. "There's a breeze coming," she announced. "It probably will get stronger too. Why don't we sail home?"

"I've had enough slow going," Bess repeated firmly. "Let's tow *Whip the Wind.*"

The sagging sail already had begun to fill. George was having difficulty keeping the boat headed into the wind.

"You see, she's begging to sail home!" Nancy laughed. "You go home in the motorboat, Bess, and take care of that sunburn. George and I will sail her home."

As Nancy and George started off, *Whip the Wind* began to sail along at a fast clip and was soon beating her way upwind on long tacks across the river.

"You certainly get the most out of this boat, Nancy," George remarked, her interest in *Whip the Wind* rapidly reviving. "I take back everything I said about her!"

"Then you think our buy wasn't so bad?"

"We ought to win the race! That is, unless you're off pursuing a mystery on regatta day."

"I'll try to arrange my schedule so that the two won't conflict," Nancy chuckled, coaxing a little more speed out of the craft. "Coming about!"

The boat made excellent time and reached River Heights shortly after the motorboat had arrived. During the next few days the three girls and a boy employed by the yacht club spent much of their time repainting *Whip the Wind*, sanding her bottom, and practising for the coming race.

Nancy also made several visits to the Struthers' home, where everything appeared to be going smoothly. Rose was bubbling with enthusiasm over her dancing and violin lessons. Her teachers had said she definitely had talent, and Mrs Struthers was highly pleased.

"Perhaps a real career in music is ahead for my grand-daughter," she said enthusiastically to Nancy when they were alone. "And I have you to thank, my dear."

"I'm glad I've done something helpful," smiled Nancy, "even though I haven't found the doll you want. But I did buy two things at the Jefferson Galleries."

She handed Mrs Struthers the package containing the four-faced doll and the album with the name of Euphemia Struthers on it.

"What an interesting doll!" the collector remarked after turning it round and round. "I haven't seen one like this before. It will be a great addition to my others. And this album—how quaint! Euphemia? Let me see. My husband had an unmarried cousin by that name."

"Where does she live?" Nancy asked eagerly.

"In some suburb of New York City. I've forgotten exactly where."

Nancy examined the album thoroughly a second time but found nothing that might help her to solve the mystery. She looked up to find Mrs Struthers with a faraway expression in her eyes.

"Could you go to New York for me?" she asked abruptly.

"New York? Why, yes, I guess so," Nancy replied. "You mean to see Euphemia Struthers?"

"If you can find her. But also to attend a large sale of exquisite old dolls," the woman said.

Nancy's mind immediately flew to various possibilities in connection with the trip. First of all, her Aunt Eloise Drew who lived in New York had been coaxing her to come for a visit; also her friend, Alice Crosby, a social worker.

"How I wish I might go myself!" sighed Mrs Struthers. "Alfred Blackwell is giving a wonderful recital."

"He is?" said Nancy. "If I go to New York, I must hear him." To herself she added, "And I'll try to have an interview with him. Being a violinist, he may have known Rose's father and can tell me where Romano is now." Aloud she said, "Yes, I'll go. When is the sale?"

"Next Wednesday."

Before leaving River Heights, Nancy decided to fill in the time profitably by trying to trail the gypsies who had broken camp near the tourist cabins where she and the girls had spent Monday night. Bess and George drove there with her and searched the community, but they could find no trace of them. The nomad tribe had disappeared as completely as if they had gone by aeroplane.

"That makes it more necessary than ever that I try to get a clue about Romano Pepito in New York," Nancy determined.

"New York?" exclaimed Bess.

Nancy explained the various reasons for the trip, and said she had decided to concentrate on finding Rose's father in the hope of learning why he had left his family so abruptly and whether he knew anything about the missing doll.

"Well, be good in the big city," George teased her as

she said goodbye. "Don't let any flat-dwelling gypsies bother you!"

Nancy grinned several times over the week-end as she thought of George's humorous warning. Talking over with Hannah what she would take on the trip, she concluded that her wardrobe could stand some additions. Consequently very few clothes were packed, for Nancy planned to spend a day shopping in the city.

She enjoyed the scenic trip on the train through the mountains. Upon arriving at the station in New York, Nancy went at once to the suburban telephone directories and looked for the name Struthers.

"Here it is!" she told herself excitedly, coming upon it. "Euphemia Struthers!"

She put in a call to the address and presently the woman herself answered.

"This is Nancy Drew from——"

"It is, eh? Well, it's about time I heard from you!" Euphemia Struthers shouted.

•11• *The Missing Musician*

NANCY was so startled by Euphemia Struthers' unexpected words that she did not even interrupt to find out if perhaps the woman had misunderstood her name.

"I thought your conscience would bother you one of these days," the tirade went on. "I want that album of mine back and I want it right away!"

Nancy was dumbfounded. The woman had not misunderstood her, then! But how had she found out that she had bought the album? A thought struck Nancy that she must have picked up some stolen property! As Miss Struthers paused for breath, she said:

"Please let me speak. I don't know how you found out I have your album, but I assure you it's in good hands. Mrs John Struthers of River Heights has it."

"What did you do with the pictures?" Euphemia screamed. "*She* hasn't got them, too! Oh, no, oh, no!"

"There weren't any in the album," said Nancy.

"What do you mean?"

Nancy at last was able to relate the whole transaction. When she finished, Miss Struthers in a greatly subdued voice asked, "Who did you say you are?"

The girl spoke her name very clearly. There came a great gasp from the telephone and a profuse apology. "Oh, my goodness, I thought you said 'Nanny Dew', that thieving maid of mine! If I ever get my hands on that girl . . ."

"Your time is up," an operator's voice cut in. "If you wish to talk longer, deposit twenty . . ."

"I don't!" said Nancy, and hung up. She leaned against the side of the telephone box and laughed merrily. "Whew! I'm glad that's over! The clue didn't get me anywhere, but I'll see that Miss Euphemia Struthers' album is returned to her. I wonder what Nanny Dew did with the photographs!"

Nancy pushed open the door of the kiosk and went directly to the taxi stand. Ten minutes later she rang the bell of her aunt's flat. Miss Drew, an attractive middle-aged woman, greeted Nancy with open arms. But as she established the girl in the guest room and helped her to unpack the few clothes she had brought along, the woman looked amazed at the scant wardrobe.

"Either you don't intend to stay long or you left home in a hurry," she teased.

"Neither. Guess again," Nancy laughed. "I'm going shopping."

"That doesn't sound like you, Nancy. Are you sure there isn't some other reason for this visit?"

"I see I can't keep secrets from you, Aunt Lou!"

Nancy explained the mystery on which she was working and her hope of tracing Romano Pepito through Alfred Blackwell, the violinist, by interviewing him after the symphony concert the next evening.

"I'll get tickets for us," Miss Drew offered at once. "And now tell me about your father and Hannah and everyone I know in River Heights."

Nancy spent a happy evening with her aunt and the next day they shopped for several hours. Nancy purchased two new dresses and also a gown and accessories to wear to the concert at which Alfred Blackwell was to be the soloist. She and Miss Drew arrived there early, and Nancy handed the usher a note to take to the violinist.

Nancy thought Blackwell's playing even more wonderful than the time she had heard him in River Heights. Just before the second half of the programme began, the usher gave Nancy an answer to her note. It invited the girl and her aunt to come backstage immediately after the concert to see the artist.

"Now if he can only give me a clue to the Struthers' mystery!" she thought excitedly.

When they met Alfred Blackwell he not only remembered having met Nancy in River Heights but expressed great pleasure that she and her aunt had come to hear him. They told him how much they had enjoyed his performance. Then, feeling it would be unfair to take many minutes of his time, Nancy explained the purpose of her request to see him.

"Romano Pepito?" Mr Blackwell repeated. "Ah, yes, I knew him. I heard him play many times. He is a fine violinist. His music expresses the depths of gloom and the heights of joy so well known to gypsies."

"Where is he now?" Nancy asked eagerly.

"That I could not say. I've not seen him for over three years. You know him?"

"No, but I'd like to meet him."

"Perhaps I can help you, if you and Miss Drew will come to my hotel tomorrow morning."

Nancy looked at her aunt, who nodded assent. At eleven o'clock the following day they went to the violinist's suite. The artist greeted them cordially but said he had disappointing news.

"I couldn't find out anything about Romano Pepito," he said. "The man seems to have vanished from the music world, though there has been no report of his death."

From a table he took a photograph and handed it to Nancy.

"A very good picture of Romano," he explained. "A handsome man, is he not?"

"This is Romano Pepito?" Nancy asked. She had not expected to see such a kind, sensitive face.

"Yes. You have never seen him?"

"No. But it's important that I find him."

"If this picture will help you any, please take it," Alfred Blackwell offered. "Romano is not in trouble?"

"Not that I know of," Nancy evasively answered. "I'm interested in all talented gypsies."

Alfred Blackwell nodded as if satisfied with the explanation. "In that case you must meet my friend Marquita," he said.

"You mean the film actress?" inquired Nancy's aunt. "She was very good in her latest film."

"Yes, her new picture is to open here this week. Marquita is a gypsy, and one of the most unselfish, beautiful women I have ever known."

"Is she in New York now?" asked Nancy.

"I believe so. Wait, I'll find out."

The violinist called a theatrical agent who arranged all

Marquita's engagements. From him he learned that the actress had arrived in the city only the day before.

"We'll go to her flat," Alfred Blackwell decided impulsively. "She has no phone or I'd call her."

They drove at once by taxi to the actress's flat. To Nancy's amazement Marquita did not reside in an exclusive neighbourhood.

"Marquita makes a large salary but spends little of it on herself," the violinist explained briefly. "I sometimes wonder if it isn't because she's compelled to turn over the major part of her earnings to the gypsy tribe of which she remains a member."

The gypsy, dark, beautiful, and exotic looking, opened the door herself. She wore plain, inexpensive clothes. Her apartment also was cheaply furnished. Marquita greeted them cordially, but before she had a chance to ask them to sit down, Mr Blackwell said enthusiastically:

"Suppose we all go to lunch! To that famous Hungarian restaurant on the next block."

Marquita offered no protest, and the Drews' objections were quickly overruled. At the restaurant Alfred Blackwell ordered a full-course meal for each one.

"This is the only time of day I have a chance to eat a square meal," he explained. "I hope you will enjoy the food here."

Nancy sought to draw Marquita into a discussion of gypsy customs and superstitions. The actress answered the questions politely but reluctantly. She could give no information about Romano Pepito and seemed disinterested in the subject of dolls or albums.

"Gypsies do not have albums," she said.

Nancy made a final attempt to get a clue from Marquita by asking whether gypsies who had been banished from a tribe could be reinstated again.

"The old tribal law is becoming more liberal," Marquita admitted. "It depends on the tribe, though. Some leaders allow certain members to go out into the world. Others allow them to leave but . . ."

"Yes?" Nancy prompted as the actress broke off.

"Others allow them to leave," Marquita repeated with finality.

Out of consideration for her host, Nancy did not pursue the subject further. The rest of the lunch hour was gay, and the guests were profuse in their thanks to Alfred Blackwell for his kindness.

The next morning Nancy and her aunt went to the sale of dolls which Mrs Struthers had mentioned. Several fine ones were on display. Many duplicated those already in the River Heights woman's collection, but one caught Nancy's fancy, and she listened attentively to a description of it when the auctioneer put the doll up for sale.

He explained that it dated back to Civil War days and had been used to carry messages and even quinine through enemy lines. He demonstrated how the head could be removed by a sudden quick turn. Beneath it was a cavity where precious drugs and notes had been secreted.

"There's a story that children were allowed to visit their fathers who were prisoners of war. They carried the dolls through the enemy lines, and no one suspected that they were helping their parents trick the enemy," he continued. " A guaranteed authentic collector's item! Now what am I offered?"

"I believe I'll buy that for Mrs Struthers' collection if the bidding doesn't go too high," Nancy whispered to her aunt.

Several persons made bids. As the price rose, everyone dropped out except Nancy and a woman at the back of the room.

"Why, she sounds like Nitaka!" Nancy thought, turning round. The woman wore a large, wide-brimmed hat which completely covered her face and hair. "Maybe she wants

that doll because it has something to do with the Struthers'
case!" Nancy reasoned excitedly.

Quickly the girl made another bid for the doll. The
woman with the veil topped her offer by a large amount.
Nancy raised the bid, but this time her competitor said
nothing, and the auctioneer called:

"Sold to the young lady in the front!"

The woman at the back of the room, muttering angrily,
left her seat and started towards the door.

"She *is* Nitaka!" Nancy decided, as the gypsy's hat
slipped to one side and revealed her carrot-coloured hair.

Nancy determined to follow her. Quickly she explained
to her aunt what she was going to do, and asked that she
wait to pay for the doll and take it home with her.

"Please be careful," Miss Drew pleaded.

"Yes, Aunt Lou. Meet you at the house."

Nancy trailed the gypsy woman to an underground
station, where she nearly lost her as she boarded a train.
Nancy dashed in just as the door closed, but when Nitaka
left the train fifteen minutes later and climbed the stairs.
to the street, she was only a little distance behind her.

The gypsy turned into a large but shabby-looking block
of flats. Nancy reached the building a few seconds later,
but could find no trace of the woman in the dimly-lit hall.

Annoyed and puzzled, she questioned a group of children
who were playing on the pavement. They had not noticed
the woman. On a sudden hunch Nancy asked them if any
gypsies lived in the building.

"Are you a lady policeman?" one of the boys demanded,
his eyes showing fright.

"No, I'm not."

"Did you come to have your fortune told?"

"If I can find a gypsy to read my palm, I will," Nancy
answered, hoping the boy could lead her to Nitaka.

"My grandmother tells fortunes," the lad declared.
"You're not a gypsy, are you?"

"Sure I am, and so's my grandmother. She tells fortunes, only the police won't let her charge anything. 'Course if you like the fortune you can give her something besides money. The police wouldn't care about that."

"I see," said Nancy. "Where is your grandmother?"

"Upstairs. Come on, I'll show you."

Leaving his playmates, the dark-eyed boy motioned for Nancy to follow him inside. Excited, she started across the pavement after him. Then she paused. Would she be running into danger if Nitaka should catch sight of her?

"Come on!" urged the boy. "My grandmother won't see anybody after twelve o'clock and it's five minutes to twelve now!"

Nancy felt that there might possibly be some connection between Nitaka and the old gypsy woman. If she did not follow this very minute, she would miss her chance!

• 12 •   *The Fortune Teller's Trick*

As NANCY hesitated for a moment, debating just what to do, someone called her name. Turning, she saw a figure in a blue suit.

"Why, Alice, where in the world did you come from?" she cried.

"Oh, Nancy, it's grand to see you again! What a wonderful surprise!" the other exclaimed.

She was Alice Crosby, the friend whom Nancy had intended to look up. The young woman said she was investigating a social work case in the neighbourhood.

"And what are *you* doing *here*?" she asked.

"I was just going to have my fortune told by a gypsy," Nancy replied with a significant wink. "Want to join me?"

Alice was quick to understand that Nancy, too, was on a case and needed help.

"You bet I'll join you. I'd love to have my fortune told, too," she winked back.

They followed the boy up the stuffy, dirty stairway to the second floor. From behind a closed door came the voices of two women quarrelling. They spoke partly in Romany, partly in English.

"We need money for the Cause, I tell you! No excuses!" one of them said cuttingly.

Nitaka!

"You are behind in your payments! I must have at least one hundred dollars!" she cried harshly.

"Oh, we are poor. We have no money," whined the other weakly. "The police stopped me from working. We can't even get enough money for food!"

"Food!" the other exclaimed. "Is not salvation for all of us more important? Give me the money!"

As Nancy listened, her pulses quickened. Why was Nitaka demanding money? What was the "Cause"?

"Wait here," said the gypsy lad, frightened. "I'll go and tell Grandmother you want your fortune told."

Before Nancy could restrain him, the boy burst through the door, shouting, "Customers!"

Instantly there was a hubbub inside. Chairs were pushed about and a door slammed. It was a few minutes before anyone appeared to greet the callers. Then a bent old woman hobbled into the outer room where Alice and Nancy stood. She had on a red flared skirt, and a yellow scarf draped completely over her head, face, and blouse.

"Hello, my pretties," she cackled in a high-pitched voice.

"We've come to have our fortunes told," Nancy said.

"You come too late," croaked the gypsy. "No longer do

I take money for telling fortunes. The police will not allow it."

"But you could accept a gift?"

"What do you offer?"

Nancy took a new, attractive compact from her bag. It would bring a good sum at a pawnshop. The gypsy's dark eyes gleamed.

"Sit down!" she ordered, pushing Nancy into a chair. "I will tell only one fortune, yours. Give me your gift."

Nancy handed the woman the compact. The gypsy took the girl's palm in her own and stared fixedly at the lines. Nancy in turn gazed down at the fortune-teller's hands, surprised to note that the flesh was as firm and hard as that of a young person.

"You do not live in New York," said the gypsy, speaking rapidly in her raspy voice. "I see you come here on a special mission to find someone. Am I right?"

Nancy pulled herself up short, realising that she had revealed by her surprised expression how accurate the woman's guess had been.

"You seek to find that which never will come to you," continued the crone. "If you value your life, you will return quickly to your home and stay there. Good times lie ahead of you—I see much money—but only if you give up your present search and cease meddling in the affairs of others!"

"Interesting," commented Nancy dryly. She decided upon a bold move. "As it happens, I came to this very house to find a woman named Nitaka. I wish to talk to her."

The gypsy's hand jerked away from her own.

"Nitaka has gone!" she muttered. Then, as an afterthought, she added, "She has not been here for a long time."

"I don't believe that," replied Nancy, "because I heard her voice a few minutes ago. She must be in this apartment!"

"Nitaka is not here!" the gypsy repeated. "You do not believe me? Then look around and let your eyes tell you so."

Nancy needed no second invitation. Opening a door to an adjoining room, she walked in, followed by Alice. Huddled in a dark corner was an old gypsy woman. She was fully dressed except for a skirt.

Instantly Nancy realised that a trick had been played on her. The fortune-teller outside was not the gypsy lad's grandmother, but Nitaka! She had put on the older woman's skirt, and had hidden her face and blouse under the scarf!

Too late, Nancy turned round. Already Nitaka was disappearing into the hall. She had stripped off the skirt and the scarf which lay on the floor.

"Stop her, Alice!" Nancy cried.

The two girls rushed to the door but Nitaka was already running down the stairway. All they could see was the top of her head. A moment later she reached the street.

"No use following her," Alice advised, pausing on the first floor.

Nancy went back to the flat to find out what she could about Nitaka from the old gypsy and the little boy. After persistent questioning, she learned that Nitaka had been there several times, trying to extort money from them.

"Why do you give her money?" Nancy asked.

"We are afraid not to," the old grandmother sighed. "Nitaka says the king of all gypsies will harm us if we do not obey her."

"I don't think you need worry any more," Nancy said kindly. "I'm sure Nitaka will not come back here to bother you, now that we've found her out." Turning to Alice, she whispered, "I think we'd better report Nitaka to the authorities."

Leaving the flat, the two girls hurried down the creaking stairs to the street.

"My, it's good to breathe fresh air again!" Alice remarked. "It was terribly smelly up there. I'll bet those rooms haven't been cleaned and aired in a long time. I must look into that situation. Those people probably need help."

"Do you know where the nearest police station is?" Nancy asked her.

Alice, familiar with that part of the city, led Nancy to one a few yards away. A pleasant officer at the desk greeted them. He remembered Alice, as he had assisted her on several of her cases. The two girls told him about Nitaka and suggested that a watch be kept for her on the chance she might return.

"I'll send a plainclothesman over there at once," he promised.

The girls thanked him and left. Nancy and Alice chatted for a while; then, after making a date to meet the next day for lunch, they parted.

As Nancy walked towards the underground station, she found herself intrigued by the shops. In the window of a small antique shop several plush-covered albums were on display. She decided to go inside and ask about them.

"It's a nuisance to get things out of the window!" complained the old man who ran the shop. "Folks always want to look, and never buy! I'm gettin' plumb tired of it!"

"I'll certainly buy an album if I find it's the kind I'm looking for," said Nancy.

Grudgingly the man got them out one by one. Observing Nancy's disappointed expression as she fingered through them, he offered her several others which he took from beneath the counter. One had a red morocco leather cover, trimmed in bands of gold leaf, with a gilt fastener. Another was of faded blue satin with an ivory clasp, and tiny yellow rosebuds painted on it.

"This old blue one contains verses," the man said. "Silly

stuff. But you could tear out the pages and put in new ones," he added practically.

The shopkeeper thumbed through the album to a passage which he scornfully read:

" 'For if kith and kin and all had sworn, I'll follow the gypsy laddie.' Now does that make sense?"

"I think it does," said Nancy, her cheeks flushed with excitement and her eyes shining. "A person might have written it who had decided to take up his lot with the gypsies. May I see the album, please?"

Unable to hide her intense eagerness, Nancy scanned the pages. On the very last one she was astounded to come across a familiar quotation. Written in bold black ink was the sentence:

The source of light will heal all ills, but a curse will follow him who takes it from the gypsies.

It was the same quotation that Mrs Struthers had found in *her* album!

Under the quotation the name *Henrietta Bostwick* appeared in tiny letters. Deeply thrilled by the discovery, Nancy turned back to the first page. A name, probably that of the original owner, had been written there, but the ink had faded and she could not decipher it.

"This album must have an interesting history," Nancy remarked to the shopkeeper. "Where did you get it?"

"Oh, it came in a barrel of stuff from another antique shop. The place was going into bankruptcy, so I took part of the stock."

Nancy bought the album and left the shop with mingled feelings of elation and defeat. Because of the strange quotation she was convinced that the unknown Henrietta Bostwick must have some connection with the Pepito family. But how could she trace her?

Passing the public library, Nancy on impulse went in. There, for two hours, she pored over records on genealogy but could find no Bostwick family listing Henrietta as a member. After she had perused all the volumes on this subject, she returned to her aunt's flat.

"Oh, Nancy, I'm so glad you've come!" Miss Drew exclaimed as her niece entered the hall. "I've been so worried."

"Worried? Why, Aunt Lou, you know I can find my way around New York without a bit of trouble."

"I haven't been worried about you, Nancy. It's a package that came."

Nancy went to look at a package lying on the table. It was addressed to her. As she reached for it her aunt cried out:

"No! No! Don't touch it!"

"Why not, Aunt Lou?"

"A woman telephoned less than half an hour ago," her aunt revealed excitedly. "She refused to give her name. But she warned me that it would be very dangerous to open the package!"

· 13 ·   *A Strange Dismissal*

NANCY looked closely at the package without touching it. Although clearly addressed to her, the sender's name did not appear, and it had not been sent by post or express delivery.

"How did it come?" she asked her aunt, puzzled.

"By the lift. Fifteen minutes after the package had been delivered the mysterious telephone call came, warning you not to open it. Oh, Nancy, we must call the police!"

"Yes," her niece agreed, reaching for the telephone.

Within a few minutes two detectives were at the flat. Clancy Brown, brusque and efficient, thought they should drop the package unopened into a bucket of water or oil.

"Might be a bomb in it for all we know," he announced.

"But there's no ticking sound," Nancy protested. "In spite of the warning, the package may be perfectly harmless. I hate to ruin the contents unless it's necessary."

"I agree with the young lady," said the other detective.

"Okay, we'll open it," Brown said, "but not here. We'll go back to the station and test it with the meter."

Nancy and her aunt went along. The girl was fascinated by the little detection gadget.

"Guess the package won't pop," said Brown. "If the contents are dangerous, it's for some other reason."

The man untied the string, and removed the heavy brown wrapping paper.

"Can't see a thing yet," he muttered. "Well, here goes!"

He raised the cover of the box an inch, peering into the crack. Then with an exclamation of disgust, he threw off the top.

"Look what's inside! Nothing but a doll! You call in the police for this!"

With a gesture of contempt, the detective started to pick it up. Nancy darted forward. Seeing the doll she cried:

"Don't touch that! It's dangerous!"

"'Dangerous? What do you mean?" Brown laughed.

"It contains a drug! This witch doll was stolen a few days ago in Jefferson."

"You're sure?"

"I never saw the doll until now," Nancy answered, "but I believe it's the one. Perhaps you'd better check with the owner of the Jefferson Galleries to make sure."

"We'll do that," Brown decided, as he replaced the box cover.

"Any idea who sent you the package, and why?" asked the other detective, looking at Nancy quizzically.

She made an evasive answer. In her own mind Nancy was satisfied that the doll was the stolen one and had been sent as an offering of ill will from Nitaka. But she had no proof, and so did not want to give the gypsy's name to the police.

Nancy wondered who could have telephoned the friendly warning. It was evident that her present address was no secret to at least two people who did not wish to make themselves known to her.

"Nitaka probably saw me in the street and followed me to Aunt Lou's apartment," she said. "But I can't imagine who my unknown friend is."

"Whoever she is, I'm thankful to her, and certainly relieved that no harm came to you," sighed Miss Drew.

Nancy spent another day in New York. Then, the following morning, despite her aunt's urgent invitation to stay a few more days, Nancy felt she should get back to River Heights to work on the mystery. She caught an afternoon plane and reached home in time for dinner. After telling her father and Hannah Gruen of her adventures, she telephoned at once to George.

"I'm back from the big city," she laughed. "How's everything?"

Nancy learned that during her absence George and Bess had faithfully sailed each day in *Whip the Wind*, but were very discouraged.

"In a light wind, we just can't coax enough speed out of her. Yesterday on the river, Phyl sailed right past us. And did she have a laugh!"

"Perhaps we need a lighter sail," suggested Nancy.

"No, I don't think that's the trouble. To tell you the truth I believe she's lonesome for you! Would you have time to make a trial run with us tomorrow?"

"I had planned to see Mrs Struthers," said Nancy. "I brought her an interesting old album with that strange 'source of light' message in it."

"Oh, really!" said George. "Well, I may have a clue for you, too. Want to know the location of a gypsy camp with a violinist?"

"Do I!"

"Then meet Bess and me at the yacht club tomorrow morning," George chuckled. "If you'll sail the boat and give us a few pointers, we'll lead you to a camp we saw the other day."

Nancy got out her car first thing the next morning and hurried to the boathouse.

"We knew you'd be interested," said Bess, as the girls prepared to shove off. "Someone was playing a violin when we sailed past the camp the other day. We didn't see who it was, but the music was beautiful."

Nancy asked a dozen eager questions, but the cousins could tell her little about the camp. They had noticed it while sailing south on Forked River on Wednesday afternoon.

"I only hope the gypsies are still there!" Nancy said, taking the tiller. "Let out the sheet a little, George. We're going places fast on this trip."

The breeze was only fair, but under Nancy's skilful handling, *Whip the Wind* began to shift faster and faster.

"I can't see anything wrong with this boat," she said, squinting up at the sail. "We're sailing perfectly."

"Nothing is wrong now," laughed Bess as she stretched herself out lazily. "All we needed was a good sailor. See to it that you don't fail us on the day of the race."

During the next half-hour Nancy made several suggestions on how to get the most out of the boat. George, taking a turn at the helm, presently cried out:

"We're coming to the camp site now. Yes, I can see tents! The gypsies are still there."

She came up to the jetty, steering sharply into the wind to lose headway. Nancy leapt out and made the boat fast to a post.

Several gypsy children who were playing nearby had seen the landing. They began chattering excitedly, and some ran off, evidently to tell their parents that visitors had arrived.

Nancy walked over to the remaining group. As the children stared at her wide-eyed, she asked if they knew a man named Romano Pepito. Soberly the children shook their heads.

Nancy took a packet of chewing gum from her pocket. "This is for the first boy or girl who tells me the name of your violinist!" she smiled.

"Murko!" cried several in unison.

Nancy split the packet of gum, so that each child got a stick. "Now lead me to Murko," she requested.

"Nobody but gypsies can see him," one little girl spoke up, frightened. "It's not allowed."

At this point a pretty woman with rings in her ears and bracelets jingling, appeared from a tent and came swiftly to the river's edge. The girls expected to be ordered to leave. Instead, the gypsy smiled and offered to tell their fortunes.

"Have you a licence to tell fortunes?" inquired Nancy.

"Yes, I have," the woman answered. She reached out as if to take the girl's hand. "Shall I read your future?"

"Oh, thank you, no. I've had my fortune told recently," Nancy replied.

Just then the strains of violin music came from one of the tents at the far end of the camp. Nancy's expression revealed her intense interest.

"I'd like to meet Murko," she said.

The gypsy looked at her intently, shook her head and whispered, "Gypsy music fills the air. Listen and you will learn. But never try to pierce their secrets, or misfortune will befall you!"

After delivering the warning, the woman turned and walked swiftly towards the cluster of tents, disappearing into one of them.

"Now what did she mean by that?" Bess asked nervously.

"I think she was telling us to move on and ask no more questions about the gypsy violinist," declared George.

"Then let's make tracks," urged Bess.

"Not so fast," Nancy pleaded. "I've not learned half enough."

She fished in the locker of *Whip the Wind*, and found several bottles of coke. Holding them up for the gypsy children to see, she called:

"Tell me, how many of you have dolls?"

All the little girls bobbed their heads.

"Show them to me, will you please, and then we'll have some coke," coaxed Nancy.

With a shout, the children ran off to the tents. Soon they returned with their treasured possessions. One quick glance, and Nancy knew none of them was the special doll Mrs Struthers wanted. Most of them were of rough, unpainted wood. One, with a wax face, had a most ludicrous expression. The wax had evidently been cracked in places by cold weather and melted in others by the sun.

"You must have lots of fun with these babies of yours," said Nancy kindly.

"They're not very pretty," one little girl spoke up. "You ought to see Nitaka's dolls! They're beautiful."

Nancy was careful to keep her voice steady as she asked, "Where is Nitaka?"

"Gone," the child said with a shrug.

"Nitaka always comes and goes," another child contributed, thirstily drinking the coke Nancy offered. "She never stays long."

"Nitaka comes and goes alone?" Nancy probed. "Sometimes, perhaps, with a man?"

"With Anton," the child with the wax doll answered.

"And Zorus? Does he live here?"

"The king of the gypsies?" the little girl said with awe. "He went——"

Before she could say any more, a bell suddenly tinkled and all the children scampered off. Nancy wondered if they had been called away purposely.

"Let's go before someone comes after us," Bess urged nervously.

At that moment the violinist began to play again, this time the *Gypsy Love Song*. The music seemed to come from the farthest tent.

"Girls, I must meet that man!" Nancy exclaimed. "He may be Romano under another name!"

"No! Don't try it!" Bess warned. "No telling what might happen to you!"

"Remember the gypsy woman's warning," added George fearfully. "Please don't . . ."

But Nancy was gone. Fearlessly she hurried towards the musician's tent.

· 14 ·   *Complications*

BEFORE Nancy could reach the tent from which the violin music was coming, a stout, ugly woman started to run towards her.

"Go!" the gypsy ordered harshly. "You are not welcome here!"

Dogs began to bark. Gypsies poured from the tents, surrounding her. Nancy found herself completely hemmed in by unfriendly faces.

"Go!" the woman shouted again. "And do not return!"

"I mean no harm," Nancy said, playing for time. "I only wish to meet the violinist."

"It is forbidden."

Nancy realised from the grim faces about her that argument was useless. Accordingly, she left and returned to the boat.

"Let's get away from here as fast as possible!" Bess pleaded as George cast off.

"The violinist probably wasn't Romano anyway," said George philosophically. "And say, I'm about starved. I think the breeze will hold. What do you say we stop at Wrightville for a bite?"

Half an hour later they tied up at the pier in the small town. Nancy brightened as they ate at a pleasant tearoom, and later went to look at the window displays of several quaint shops. One antique shop with dolls in the window drew her attention. As she started to cross the street to it, a man came out of the shop, clasping a small bundle against his coat pocket. Startled, Nancy said to her friends:

"Girls, there's the pick-pocket!" She darted after him. "Come on! We mustn't let him get away this time!"

The fellow, seeing that Nancy had recognised him, ran to the corner where a bus had just stopped. He jumped inside, and a second later the vehicle pulled away from the kerb.

"We must follow it!" Nancy told the other girls, looking round for a taxi.

There was not a cab in sight. Inquiring of the driver of a parked car the way to a garage where a taxi might be hired, the girls learned there was one farther down the street. Hearing that they were trailing a thief, he offered to drive them to the garage.

"Sorry I can't chase the bus myself," he said.

The only taxi at the garage was an old, dilapidated one with room for only two passengers.

"I'll wait here," offered Bess.

"I don't think I can overtake that bus," the driver said, after Nancy told him what they wanted. "It's got too much of a start. But I can try."

From the outset, the chase was hopeless. They drove for a few miles without even catching a glimpse of the bus. Aware that the cab fare was mounting to no purpose, Nancy finally told the driver to turn back. In town once more, they found Bess.

"Who says I'm not a super detective?" she giggled. "While you girls were gone, I went to the antique shop where we saw the pick-pocket and got some information about him."

"What was it?" Nancy asked eagerly.

"The pick-pocket sold a doll to the dealer for one hundred and fifty dollars!"

"Did you see the doll, Bess?" Nancy asked excitedly.

"Yes, it was an Early American rag doll. Its hands were made of old kid gloves and it had shoe buttons for eyes. The dealer said that the face had been painted on with vegetable dyes. For the life of me, I can't see why anyone would pay such a fancy price for a rag doll!"

"Because they're so rare," Nancy explained.

"It was kind of cute at that," said Bess. "The doll's hair was made of yellow string. Its dress was an India print skirt with a little homespun linen jacket."

"Girls, that thief may have stolen it from Mrs Struthers!" cried Nancy. "I remember seeing one like it in her collection."

"The pick-pocket was carrying a package with him when he left the shop," George reminded the others. "What do you suppose was in it? Something else he stole?"

"The shopkeeper said the man had another doll with him to sell," Bess explained, "but the dealer didn't want to buy it."

Nancy decided to telephone Mrs Struthers at once to find out whether the doll just purchased by the antique dealer belonged to her. But when she described the doll, Mrs Struthers said it did not belong to her collection.

"I have one exactly like it except for the India print dress," Mrs Struthers said. "My doll is safe. The one which was sold must be——"

Before Mrs Struthers could continue, Rose cut in on an extension telephone and excitedly began to tell Nancy of her music and dancing lessons.

"Oh, I just love them!" she shouted. "My teacher says I'm a 'natural'. I'm to have an audition for the radio or films if Granny will say it's okay."

"Granny hasn't said so yet," Mrs Struthers interrupted. "Rose is not doing so well with her other lessons, Nancy, and until she does I couldn't think of such a thing."

"I can't study all the time!" Rose exclaimed. "Anyway, it's just like being in jail here! I can't leave the house without being watched!"

"Why, what do you mean?" cried Mrs Struthers.

"I know you put a detective on the grounds. He watches me all the time! I don't like it! Everybody in this house is being watched."

Dismayed that Rose had learned about the detective whom Mr Drew had employed, Nancy tried to calm her and her grandmother, who, of course, professed her innocence in the matter.

"Please don't worry," Nancy pleaded. "I'm responsible for this, and I'll explain everything when I see you."

Alarmed at the turn affairs had taken, Nancy and her friends went back to the boat and set sail for home. The boat performed well, but the wind was not favourable. As a result, several hours elapsed before Nancy reached the Struthers home.

Arriving there, she learned her telephone call had caused much confusion in the household. Rose's conversation had been overheard by the housekeeper, Mrs Carol, who had promptly repeated it to her husband.

Convinced that a detective had been employed because the couple was thought to be dishonest, the woman had announced they were leaving at once. To pacify them, Mrs Struthers had ordered the detective off the grounds.

Nancy's explanation of why her father had engaged the man without first speaking to Mrs Struthers cleared matters somewhat. The woman said she appreciated their good intentions, but did not want the detective to return.

"I've brought some purchases, and also a photograph of Romano Pepito," said Nancy.

The woman's eyes opened wide. "I've never seen a picture of him. Is he——?"

Nancy smiled as she handed over the picture. "He's very handsome, and kind looking. I'm sure he wouldn't harm anyone intentionally. No doubt he was forced to leave his family against his will."

Mrs Struthers gazed at the photograph for several seconds before speaking. Tears filled her eyes. "I—I do so wish things had been different," she said. "Yes, he is handsome. Rose looks like him and no doubt inherits his musical talent. But the fire in her——"

"What fire?" asked a sudden voice, and Rose danced into the room. Seeing the photograph, she cried out, "Who's this? Don't tell me! I know! It's my father!"

"What makes you think so?" Nancy countered, giving Mrs Struthers a chance to decide whether to tell her grand-daughter the truth.

"Because I look like him!" said Rose.

Nancy glanced at Mrs Struthers, who was gazing affectionately at the girl. "Yes, he is your father," she said quietly.

"I want to see him!" Rose cried excitedly. "Take me to him!"

"We do not know where he is—or do you, Nancy?" the woman asked hopefully.

Nancy shook her head.

"Oh, please find him," Rose begged.

"I'm trying to," said the young detective, smiling kindly at the eager girl.

As Rose claimed the picture for herself and went off with it, Nancy explained to Mrs Struthers how she had obtained the photograph and what she was doing to try to locate Romano Pepito.

"Have you ever heard of a Henrietta Bostwick?" she asked.

"No," the woman answered as Nancy opened the package with the old album in it, and showed her the strange message which was a duplicate of the one in her own album.

The source of light will heal all ills, but a curse will follow him who takes it from the gypsies.

"What a coincidence!" exclaimed Mrs Struthers. "I've never heard of the woman."

"This Henrietta Bostwick may have sent the same quotation to your daughter."

"That's so!" agreed Mrs Struthers.

She and Nancy discussed the mystery from various angles, but arrived at no definite conclusion. Nancy then told her how she had chased a man in Wrightville whom she thought was the pick-pocket.

"Sorry I didn't catch him," she said.

"Oh, Nancy, I meant to tell you," Mrs Struthers interrupted. "The police telephoned this morning. The pick-pocket's name is known."

"It is?"

"Yes, they believe he's Tony Wassell, a half-breed gypsy. Following the tip given by the guard at the museum the police traced him through bank records."

"So Tony Wassell is a half-breed gypsy," Nancy remarked thoughtfully. "I'll bet he steals and sells valuable old dolls as well as other things, and hides in a nearby gypsy camp. I'll tell the state police that!" She telephoned the information at once as to where she had seen him and her idea about where he might be found.

"If only the man could be captured before he has a chance to use the information contained in the bag!" Mrs Struthers continued when Nancy came back.

"You mean he might blackmail you or rob you?" Nancy asked.

"Yes. Oh, I never wanted anyone but Rose to see the letter, and not until after my death. That was why I always carried it with me."

Mrs Struthers did not explain further and Nancy politely did not question her.

"Some nights I can't sleep, worrying about what may happen," Mrs Struthers went on. "Some gypsies are such vindictive creatures. I've been told that if their tribal laws are violated by one of their number, they often seek revenge on a member of the family. I'm fearful that they may try to harm Rose because her father married outside his tribe."

"Please try not to worry about it," Nancy said, not telling that this very idea had been plaguing her for some time.

The next Monday morning, when Nancy came down to breakfast, she found her father and Hannah Gruen had already eaten. The mail had come, and at her place on the dining-room table lay two letters.

One of them was postmarked Wrightville, and her name and address had been printed in a strange way, as if the sender did not wish his identity known. Puzzled, Nancy tore open the envelope. It bore only a single sheet of cheap paper with this warning message:

"Stay at home, Nancy Drew, and attend to your own business! If you don't, it will be the worse for you!"

·15· *A Warning*

HANNAH GRUEN, coming into the dining room, knew from Nancy's expression that something was wrong.

"What is it?" she cried. "Not bad news, I hope."

Nancy showed her the warning note. "I can't imagine who could have sent it," she said, "unless it was the pickpocket."

"Oh, Nancy, I'm so worried!" the housekeeper exclaimed after she had read the anonymous message. "It must have something to do with the case you're working on. Please give up trying to help Mrs Struthers!"

"I can't let a little note like this frighten me," said Nancy. "Anyway, I think the person who sent it merely means he wants me to stay away from Wrightville."

"Then promise me you will," begged Hannah Gruen.

"All right," Nancy laughed, giving the housekeeper an affectionate hug. "By the way, any telephone calls for me while I was in the shower?"

"One from the yacht club. A friend of yours said she was to let you know about picking up some clothes over there."

"Oh, yes," Nancy said absently. "I got a new locker and left some things in the old one. Well, I'll run out and get them now."

"Do be careful," Mrs Gruen urged, as Nancy went out of the door.

"I'll be all right," Nancy called cheerily, as she hopped into her car.

She drove over the heavy bridge that spanned the

Muskoka River, and headed for the yacht club, a few miles below River Heights. The river road was practically deserted.

Suddenly Nancy noticed another car a short distance behind her. Though she deliberately slowed down for it to pass, the driver did not attempt to do so. She accelerated her pace. The man behind also put on speed.

"He's following me!" Nancy decided finally. "Maybe there's more to that warning note than I thought!"

She kept the image of the other car in her mirror, and as she neared a sharp and dangerous turn where the road shot up a hill, she was alarmed to see that the driver behind her was getting closer and closer.

Although she forced her car's engine to its utmost, Nancy could not draw away from the pursuing car. A quarter of a mile from the clubhouse it pulled abreast of her. But the man did not try to head Nancy off. Instead, he crowded her inch by inch towards the embankment.

Nancy's heart stood still!

Just then her eyes spied an opening in the low bushes along the right side of the road fifty feet ahead. She recalled that from there a narrow path ran off at an angle down to the river. It was steep and hardly wide enough for a car, but she must risk taking the path if she could only reach it.

"I must hold on until I do!" Nancy thought desperately. "Then I can jump out and run!"

Forty more feet to go! Then thirty!

The two cars were neck and neck. Nancy did not dare take her eyes from the road to see who the man alongside her might be.

Twenty feet! Ten!

Suddenly Nancy swung the wheel over. Her car swerved off the road, bumped over the uneven side road and, still upright, jerked to a stop. Grabbing the key, Nancy jumped out and ran like a deer towards the yacht club.

A few seconds later she halted. The other driver, taken completely by surprise, had seemed on the verge of bringing his own car to a stop and pursuing her. Then he appeared to decide against this plan, for he resumed speed and was fast disappearing from sight.

The car was a black saloon!

Quivering, Nancy sat down on the path to recover from the shock and think things over. Finally she gave up trying to figure out who the man was. Getting to her feet, she returned to her car and tried to back it on to the road, but the wheels merely spun round in the loose earth.

"I'll have to get someone to give me a push," she decided.

After locking the car, Nancy walked swiftly down the path to the yacht club. Near the club-house she spied John Holden, an elderly man who did odd jobs on the grounds, and was particularly friendly to the young people.

"Hello, John," she greeted him. "My car's stuck up on the hill. Any chance of getting some of the men to push it out?"

"Sure thing, Miss Nancy!" he replied with a grin. "My, but you got out here fast after I phoned."

"After you phoned?"

"Sure, about your boat."

Nancy was mystified. "I didn't get your call," she said.

"Then you ain't heard the bad news? I told that house-keeper o' your'n, but I reckon you were already on your way out here."

"What about my boat?" Nancy asked, worried. "She didn't break away?"

"Worse'n that," the old man reported. "She's sunk at the dock—just bein' held up by her bow and stern lines."

Nancy was aghast. "You mean—she sprang a leak?"

"It ain't a leak. She's got a hole stove in her bow big as my fist. You'll have to haul 'er out and have a new plank put in 'er."

Nancy took the blow in silence and followed John to

the jetty. As he had said, *Whip the Wind*, held by her two lines, was under water.

"Better git her out quick as you kin," the old man advised. "Bein' under water ain't doin' the mahogany no good."

"When did this happen?" Nancy asked, her voice grim.

"Must 'a been sometime during the night."

"Did anyone take her out without permission?"

"Not so far's I know. The caretaker sleeps in the buildin' all night. He said he didn't see no boats out late."

"There wasn't much wind last night," Nancy thought aloud. "*Whip the Wind* was securely tied and couldn't have suffered that damage in her bow merely by bumping against the jetty wall."

"Looks to me like it was done on purpose," the man said. "It's sure a shame, with the race comin' on and all. Reckon this will put you out o' the runnin' unless you kin git another boat."

"Maybe I can get a quick repair job done at the Foster Boat Works," Nancy said hopefully.

"They're filled up with work for three weeks ahead."

"I'll find someone," Nancy vowed. "But the first thing is to have *Whip the Wind* hoisted out of the water. Oh, how I hate to tell the other girls about this!"

Using the yacht-club telephone, she called Bess and George. They took the news stoically, but George agreed with John that someone must have damaged the boat deliberately.

Nancy spent the next half hour telephoning various places to find a boat repair yard which would take on the job. After being turned down by several of them, she recalled an old man she had known since childhood, Sam Pickard, who ran a small repair shop.

"Well, Nancy, seein' it's you, I'll take your boat and put her ahead of my other work," he agreed. "But I'm tellin' you, it'll be a hard job to get her ready in time for the race."

"You'll make it, I'm sure," Nancy smiled. "And thank you."

"I ain't promisin'," the old boat builder said gloomily. "Furthermore, if the hole's as bad as you say, your boat ain't goin' to be very fast again even if we do fix 'er up."

"Well, do the best you can," Nancy sighed.

By the time she returned to *Whip the Wind*, Bess and George had arrived at the club. Furious at what had happened, George wanted to know who had done such a mean thing and why.

"I don't know, George," Nancy replied. "I suspect, though, it was someone who wants to distract my mind from the Struthers case. Today I received a warning message, and on the way here a man in a black saloon forced me off the road. I almost went over the cliff!"

"Oh, Nancy!" cried Bess. "It makes me shiver even to think of it! Maybe he was that awful pick-pocket getting revenge!"

"I didn't realise things were that serious," George said, also frightened. "But if anyone's trying to keep you at home by warnings and sunken boats, he doesn't know you!"

"What about *Whip the Wind*?" asked Bess.

"I've given the repair job to Sam Pickard," Nancy replied. "He hopes to have her ready in time for the race."

"We'll have no chance to practise," wailed George. "If I could only find out who stove that hole in the boat, I'd——"

George did not finish her belligerent remark because just then John brought two other club employees to push Nancy's car back to the main road.

"I believe I'll go on home," Nancy said to the other girls as she started off with the men. "See you soon."

It was only after considerable effort that the men managed to get the car up the hill. They warned Nancy to drive slowly in case any damage had been done to it. However, everything seemed to work perfectly.

When she reached her home some time later, Hannah

said, "Did you get the message about the boat?"

"Yes," Nancy replied ruefully and told about the hole in it.

"There was another call for you, too," said the housekeeper. "A woman who didn't leave her name said she had something very important to tell you, and would call you again in a little while."

Nancy, wondering if it had anything to do with the mystery, busied herself about the house to wait for the second message. Perhaps the caller was the woman who had kept her from being harmed by the witch doll. Or she might be another enemy! As the hours slipped by and the telephone did not ring, Nancy told Hannah she thought the message might have been a ruse to keep her at home.

"Well, I'm just as glad," said the housekeeper. "Please heed the warning. Don't invite trouble by going out again today. Why don't you work on the mystery from here?"

"A good idea," agreed Nancy, still thinking of her narrow escape in the car. "I'll try solving it from this big overstuffed chair."

She curled up in her father's favourite chair and thoughtfully gazed into space. She went over the puzzle piece by piece. Finally her mind reverted to the several bands of gypsies she had encountered and the strange actions of their leaders.

"There must be some definite meaning behind it all. Take that woman in the camp by the river, for instance. She wasn't unfriendly, yet she uttered that queer phrase:

" '*Gyspy music fills the air. Listen and you will learn.*'

"What was she trying to tell me? Was she answering my question about Romano Pepito, perhaps?" Suddenly, as if the young detective's subconscious mind had solved the riddle, an answer came to her.

" '*Gypsy music fills the air!*' " she exclaimed. "Why, maybe that woman meant the radio! Maybe Romano Pepito plays over the air!"

Nancy eagerly studied the radio programmes listed in the newspaper, but she could find no station offering any gypsy music. Refusing to be discouraged, she telephoned several nearby broadcasting stations to ask whether a gypsy violinist ever played on their programmes. The answer each time was no.

Nancy was not willing to give up her search yet. Obtaining a list of stations within a two-hundred-mile radius of River Heights, she sat down to write a note of inquiry to each one.

As she wrote, the girl kept the radio on, absently listening to a serial story. The programme ended and another began. Presently a violinist started to play the *Hungarian Rhapsody*.

Nancy dropped her pen to listen. The abandon of his style fascinated her. Suddenly she realised that only recently she had heard the selection played with the same interpretation. But where? Then she remembered.

"At the gypsy camp!" she recalled excitedly. "Maybe this is the same violinist and I'll hear his name!"

But at the end of the programme no name was announced. Jumping up, Nancy raced to the telephone to call the broadcasting station.

·16·   *The Ransacked House*

IN A moment, Nancy had the station on the telephone. Eagerly she inquired the name of the violinist who had just played the *Hungarian Rhapsody*.

"Alfred Dunn," came the polite reply.

"He's a gypsy, isn't he?" Nancy asked.

"Indeed not. Thank you for calling. Please keep listening to our programmes." The girl hung up.

"Another disappointment," sighed Nancy, but added hopefully, "Maybe I'll hear something from one of these letters."

She finished them, and was about to start for the corner post-box, when the telephone rang. Ned Nickerson was calling.

"How about seeing you tomorrow night, Nancy?" he asked. "Say about eight o'clock? The crowd wants to go to the Crow's Nest."

"I'd love to go. You always cheer me up, and I guess I need some cheering right now with another failure on this mystery of mine."

By the next morning Nancy's mood was cheerful again. She joked with her father at breakfast, and after he left the house, opened the newspaper to glance at the radio programmes. As she turned the pages, an advertisement caught her eye. After reading it twice, she said to Hannah Gruen:

"Please don't ask me to stay at home again today. Here's something I *must* follow up."

"What is it?"

"There's an advert telling about a chain of toy agencies in towns around here," Nancy replied. "They lend toys and also repair them. Maybe they have old dolls——"

"And you can find a solution to the Struthers mystery!" supplied Hannah good-naturedly. "All right, go ahead, but stay on the main roads."

The rest of the day Nancy spent driving from one shop to another. In each place she looked for a doll which lit up or wore a jewelled robe. The managers had neither seen nor heard of any that fitted this description.

Finally Nancy came to a small shop in the town of Malvern. As she entered, a retired dollmaker, Mr Hobnail, glanced up from a toy train he was repairing. On the workbench were many dolls and other toys awaiting attention.

"Yes?" he inquired in a weary voice. "If it's repairing you want done, I can't touch it for two weeks. I'm head over heels in work now."

Nancy told him of her interest in old dolls. As she spoke, her eyes circled the cluttered little room, coming to rest upon the toy figure of a man holding part of a violin.

"That doll!" she exclaimed suddenly. "Tell me, please, where did you get it?"

Old Mr Hobnail scarcely looked up from his work. "Woman named Mrs Barlow," he answered briefly. "Fixin' that violin's to be my next job."

"Have you her address?"

"Certainly," the old man snapped. "I always keep addresses of all my customers. She lives at the corner of Beech and Chestnut avenues."

Nancy felt that the doll might be the one Nitaka had carried in the suitcase which had fallen open, revealing its contents to Janie and the other children. After thanking the man, Nancy drove at once to the home of Mrs Barlow. She proved to be a pleasant person, and willingly told Nancy how she had obtained the doll.

"I bought it from a woman who came to my house," Mrs Barlow said. "Not until she had gone did I notice that the little violin was about to come apart, so I took it to Mr Hobnail."

"Do you know the woman's name?"

"She didn't give it to me."

"Please tell me what you remember about her."

"She was a very vivid individual—well-groomed and wore a tailored suit. Her skin was dark, but her hair was, well, I guess you'd call it carrot-coloured."

"She must have been a gypsy named Nitaka!" Nancy exclaimed. "I know she had such a doll."

"Who is Nitaka?"

Nancy told a little of what she knew about the gypsy, hinting that she might be a thief.

"Oh, dear!" Mrs Barlow became worried. "I hope I haven't bought a stolen doll!"

"Not necessarily," Nancy reassured her. "I do wish I could find that woman, though."

Mrs Barlow suddenly brightened. "I just thought of something. That gypsy said she might come back again tonight with another doll!"

"What time?" asked Nancy excitedly.

"About seven-thirty. Why don't you come?" Mrs Barlow invited. "We'll have dinner together."

Nancy did not like to impose upon the woman's good nature, but felt she probably had hit on something important. She accepted the invitation, and returned to her home in order to change into a maxi-dress for the dance. She then telephoned Ned's parents and left word for him to call for her at the Barlow home. Not wishing to have Nitaka see her car, she parked it in the Barlow garage.

The dinner was a pleasant occasion for Nancy, because she found Mrs Barlow's conversation very interesting. At ten minutes to eight the doorbell rang. The woman answered it, confidently expecting the gypsy. The caller was not Nitaka, but Ned.

Nancy presented the young man to Mrs Barlow and told him about the expected visitor, and he willingly agreed to postpone taking Nancy to the Crow's Nest. The evening wore on. By nine-thirty it became evident that Nitaka was not coming.

"Something must have made her afraid to come back," Nancy said.

To wait longer seemed useless, so Nancy and Nèd bade Mrs Barlow good-night and started out. Since each of them had a car, Ned suggested that Nancy go ahead of him, so he could keep an eye out for anyone who might try to harm her. Nothing happened, however, and presently they arrived at the Crow's Nest, the special rendezvous of River Heights young people. Nancy and Ned joined one of the friendly groups, and ordered cokes.

News had gone around that Nancy was absorbed in another mystery. Though she did not deny this, she evaded revealing any details of the case on which she was working. Ned was not so secretive.

"If you ask me, Nancy's reverting to her childhood!" he declared teasingly. "Dolls are now one of her big interests!"

"But I don't play with them," Nancy laughed.

"That's a mystery," Ned countered.

During the conversation Dot Larken remarked that the River Heights Yacht Club was having a big-little sister picnic at Star Island the next day.

"You're coming, aren't you, Nancy?" she asked.

Nancy had forgotten about the picnic. After a little urging, she said, "Yes, I'll come and bring a girl named Rose Struthers."

Unnoticed, in the adjoining booth a swarthy couple sat quietly eating ice cream. At the mention of Rose's name, they exchanged significant glances but said nothing. They remained in the booth until after Nancy and her friends had left the Crow's Nest.

The next day was sunny and warm, perfect weather for the picnic. Convinced that Rose would enjoy the outing, Nancy prevailed upon Mrs Struthers to allow her granddaughter to go.

"This is my first day out of jail," Rose grinned as they drove to the yacht club to take the boat to Star Island.

"You'd better not say things like that at the picnic or people will believe you," Nancy cautioned her laughingly.

At first Rose behaved surprisingly well, and Nancy felt that the training she had suggested was having a good

effect. Rose entertained the group with a series of remark-
ably well-executed dances, which showed real talent.

"My teacher's arranging for radio and film auditions
for me," she said boastfully.

"Come, Rose," Nancy broke in, and took the girl off
for a swim.

Rose, though not a good swimmer, was utterly fearless
in the water. Ignoring a request from Nancy not to go into
deep water, she struck out for a float. Nancy brought her
back to the beach,

When the older girl turned to speak to a friend, Rose
again struck out for deep water. Suddenly she disappeared.
Three small girls on shore who had been watching screamed
in terror. Nancy plunged into the water to search
for her. A second later Rose bobbed up, laughing glee-
fully.

"Scared you, didn't I?" she shouted. "I was just holding
my breath."

When the picnic was over they started for Rose's home.
Upon reaching the Struthers house, Rose rang the
front doorbell. To their amazement no one came to let
them in.

"Where is everybody?" Nancy asked, wondering why
neither of the servants answered the bell.

"It *is* funny," said Rose. "But I know where to find a key.
Come on!"

Darting around to a side porch, she found the key
behind a shutter and unlocked the door to the room where
the doll collection was kept. She pushed it open, then stopped
short.

"Why, look at the furniture!" she exclaimed. "It's all
topsy-turvy!"

Nancy peered through the doorway. Chairs had been
pushed out of place. Drawers had been emptied on the
floor. The doll cabinet stood open and there were many
vacant spaces on the shelves.

"The house has been robbed!" Nancy cried.

"And something awful's happened to my grandmother!" screamed Rose.

• 17 • *An Interrupted Programme*

FOR A moment Nancy thought Rose had seen Mrs Struthers, but this was not the case.

"Granny said she was going to stay home all day!" Rose cried fearfully. "Maybe those awful people came and took her away!"

Nancy did not comment. She and Rose ran through the lower part of the house searching and calling for Mrs Struthers and the servants. No one answered.

"Listen!" commanded Nancy suddenly.

From upstairs came a muffled cry that sounded like a call for help. Taking the steps two at a time, the girls rushed to Mrs Struthers' bedroom.

The door was locked. As Nancy twisted the knob in vain, she again heard the cry.

"Is that you, Mrs Struthers?" she called loudly.

"Yes! Yes! Let me out!" came a faint cry.

"Oh, what's happened to Granny?" wailed Rose.

"There's no key in the door!" Nancy shouted.

She could not understand the reply, but Rose darted across the hall and took a key from the door of another room.

"This'll open it," she said.

Quickly Nancy unlocked Mrs Struthers' door. The woman was locked in a cupboard, but the same key fitted that door, too, and she was soon released. Clad in a blue house-coat, her hair untidy, she stumbled out. Nancy helped her to the bed.

"Have they gone?" Mrs Struthers asked wildly.

"The burglars? Yes. Perhaps you'd better not talk now," Nancy suggested, seeing how white and nervous she was.

"I'm—I'm all right, but what a fright!" Mrs Struthers said. "Did they—take much?"

Rose spoke up. "A lot of the dolls. Oh, Granny, why did the thieves lock you up?"

"So that I couldn't call the police, I guess."

"Where is Mrs Carol?" Nancy asked.

"Everyone has gone away. Oh, I see it all now! It was a trick! First, someone called to say Mrs Carol was wanted at the home of a sick relative. Her husband drove her there in the car."

"Did you see the intruders, Mrs Struthers?" Nancy asked.

"Only one, but from their voices I know there were two men."

"Please tell me exactly what happened."

"I was in my room taking a nap when I heard footsteps in the hall. At first I thought Mrs Carol had come back. Then I got up to make certain. Before I knew what was happening, a man with his face covered came in and locked me in the cupboard. Oh, it was dreadful!"

"How long were you in there, Granny?" Rose asked, still frightened by what had happened.

"Easily half an hour. I'd have smothered if it hadn't been for the opening above the door."

"Then the burglars haven't been gone long," Nancy surmised. "Let's see what's been stolen," she suggested.

Going from room to room, Mrs Struthers made a hasty inspection. Silverware and jewellery had been taken; but what upset her most was that all the gems had been removed from the cover of the treasured family album.

When she saw the doll cabinet Mrs Struthers gave a cry of distress. Making a quick count, she estimated that at least twenty of her most valuable dolls were gone.

"My mummy's doll is missing!" cried Rose angrily. "The one she played with when she was a little girl."

"Yes, they took that, too," her grandmother said, gazing sadly at the shelf where the doll had stood. "Now why would they steal that one? It had no re-sale value."

Mrs Struthers' last remark set Nancy thinking. She suspected that the burglars might have been Anton and another gypsy; perhaps the pick-pocket Tony Wassell. Though they obviously had taken jewels, silverware and rare dolls to sell, it did seem odd that they also had selected the one belonging to Rose's mother.

"Perhaps it may turn out to be a helpful clue in solving the mystery," Nancy remarked thoughtfully.

At this moment a key turned in the front door. For a moment the three in the house were fearful of more trouble, but the newcomers proved to be the housekeeper and her husband. They were amazed to hear about the robbery, but declared it explained the reason for the fake telephone call.

At Nancy's insistence, Mrs Struthers got in touch with the police and reported her loss. A few minutes later two detectives arrived at the house.

Nancy, feeling she could do nothing more for Mrs Struthers, returned to her own home. Coming into the front hall, she saw the afternoon mail on the table. One of the letters was addressed to her. Noting the name Radio Station KIO, Winchester, on the envelope, she eagerly ripped it open.

"This must be an answer about the gypsy violinist!" she thought excitedly.

The programme director of the small Winchester station had written that a violinist would broadcast the following evening at eight o'clock.

"The man may be a gypsy," he wrote. "In fact, we suspect that he is, though he uses the name Albert Martin. We suggest if you are interested in obtaining additional information, you write to him at our station."

"I'll go there!" Nancy decided. "Dad will take me. This is what I call a lucky break."

Unfortunately Mr Drew had to go out of town and could not attend the broadcast, but Ned called, saying he did not have to stay at the boys' camp that evening and would like to see Nancy.

"Let's go to Winchester," she said, and explained her reason.

Scarcely half an hour later, Mrs Barlow telephoned to say she had been down to Mr Hobnail's shop, and had seen a doll there which might have some significance for Nancy.

"It's really a mannequin, but it's only twenty-six inches high," she said. "Mr Hobnail says it's one of a collection that's carried from place to place. I thought it just possible it might belong to some tribe of gypsies."

Nancy thanked the woman, saying she certainly would look at the mannequin doll. Then she asked if the red-haired gypsy had called at the house again. Mrs Barlow said she had not heard from her.

She also told Nancy that Mr Hobnail was to be in his shop late that evening, so Nancy asked Ned to stop there with her on their way to Winchester. When they reached the toy shop and Nancy told Mr Hobnail what she had come to see, he led the way to the back of the shop.

"Well, there's the mannequin. Had to get my wife to put all these fine clothes back on her," he chuckled.

The elderly man pointed to a doll about two feet high, dressed as a bridesmaid. She wore a pale blue gown with a bouffant tulle skirt, and a large picture hat. Nancy, though intrigued by the doll's charm, felt sure she was too typically American to belong to any gypsies.

"She looks almost real," Nancy said admiringly. "Where did you get her, Mr Hobnail?"

"A young man brought her in to have one of the arms repaired. He said there's a whole set of these dolls dressed like a wedding party—the bride, the groom, and the whole works!

"He's a salesman for some dress manufacturer, I believe," Mr Hobnail went on. "Goes around giving exhibitions with his lady dolls. They're to be shown at Taylor's Department Store in River Heights in a couple of days if you want to see 'em."

"I must go," said Nancy.

Secretly she was disappointed that the mannequin had no connection with her own quest. Ned reminded her that time was slipping away, so they left at once.

"We'll have to step on it to get to Winchester by eight," Ned said, looking at the car clock.

"It'll be my own fault if we don't get to the broadcast in time," Nancy remarked, "but I hope we can make it."

Ned drove as fast as the law allowed. It was just eight o'clock when the young people reached the KIO building.

Nancy was fearful that they would not be permitted to watch the broadcast, as the programme already was on the air. But a young woman at a desk directed them to a small room with a large window through which they could look down into the studio where Mr Martin, the violinist, was playing. To Nancy's surprise, she and Ned were his only audience.

"That violinist does look like a gypsy," Nancy thought, as they seated themselves. "But he's not Romano."

Nevertheless, she decided to speak to him later and ask him if he knew Rose's father. As she listened attentively to an exquisite number from *The Gypsy Airs*, the girl thought to herself:

"I hope Hannah is listening at home. It would be a shame for her to miss this beautiful music."

Back in River Heights, Mrs Gruen was indeed listening. For ten minutes she had sat near the radio, growing more entranced each moment.

"That man is too great an artist not to be playing on a nation-wide broadcast," she said, half aloud. "I'm amazed he—oh!"

The violinist had struck a sharp discord. On a high, squeaking note, the playing suddenly ceased. Angrily a voice cried out:

"Murko will play no more! I will not have spies watching me! You play trick——"

Abruptly the programme was cut off the air!

· 18 ·   *A Strange Present*

AT THE broadcasting studio, Nancy and Ned were even more startled than Hannah Gruen. In the midst of a beautiful passage, the gaze of the musician suddenly focused upon them. His eyes blazed. He struck a discord and stopped playing. Pointing his bow at Nancy, he cried out:

"Murko will play no more! I will not have spies watching me! You play trick . . ."

Murko the gypsy violinist! In his excitement "Mr Martin" had blurted out his real name!

At this moment the programme was cut off in the control room. Murko stumbled from the studio. Nancy, too, rushed outside and down a stairway, followed by Ned. On the floor below, the musician was gesticulating wildly with his bow at the studio director, who had come to find out what had happened.

"You break promise to me!" Murko shouted at the man. "When I sign to play here, you promise no one ever see me! Only hear me! And now, two people in studio . . . spies! They follow me now!"

The violinist pointed accusingly at Nancy and Ned, now in the hallway.

"Take it easy, Mr Martin," said the director. "I did not know anyone was watching you. But these people meant no harm, I'm sure."

"They come to make trouble!" the musician exclaimed wrathfully. "I told Anton if I played over radio, some day I get caught!"

"We're not here to harm you," Nancy said. "We just wanted to see you play. One misses so much not watching a great artist like youself!"

At these words of praise, Murko calmed down somewhat. Nevertheless, he moved along the hallway, a furtive look in his black eyes.

"Let us drive you to your home, Mr Martin," Nancy suggested, purposely using his radio name.

"No!" shrieked the man, apparently frightened anew.

"I believe we can help you," Nancy said kindly.

"What can you do for me?" he demanded suspiciously. "There is no help for poor Murko. None."

"Why do you say that?" Nancy asked. As he did not answer, she said, "Is it because you work so hard and are forced to give all your money to Anton and Nitaka?" Murko still remained silent. "You are discouraged because all your earnings must go to the Cause?"

Murko's head dropped. "Yes," he muttered bitterly. "Yes, it is so."

"Why don't you refuse to contribute? Surely you realise there's nothing in it for you . . . any more than for Marquita or Romano Pepito."

Murko raised his head, looking straight into Nancy's

eyes. "No, there is not. Poor Romano," he murmured. "A man broken in spirit."

Nancy's heart started to pound. Was she on the verge of learning about Rose's father?

"Where is Romano now?" she asked.

"Wherever his tribe is . . . unless they have moved him as they did me."

"What do you mean?" Nancy asked, puzzled.

Murko did not reply. A look of panic suddenly came over his face. As if frightened at having told the visitors too much, he bolted for a lift which had stopped at that floor. He dashed in and the door slammed shut.

By the time Nancy and Ned had descended to the ground floor in another lift, Murko was nowhere to be seen. No one could tell them which direction he had taken.

"Guess he gave us the slip," said Ned, disgusted. "If I'd only been quicker . . ."

"It wasn't your fault, Ned," Nancy consoled him, and added, "at least I've found out why the gypsies at that river camp wouldn't let anyone see Murko. To the outside world, he is 'Mr Martin'."

Thinking perhaps he had fled to his tribesmen, the young people inquired at the local police station if there were any gypsies in the vicinity. They were told of a camp approximately ten miles distant, off the Woodville Road. Nancy wondered if the group from the carnival was there.

"Murko probably is with them, and maybe Anton and Nitaka," she declared to Ned. "Let's try to find the place."

"We're off!" said Ned.

Police directions on how to reach the camp had been somewhat sketchy, the couple soon discovered. To find the Woodville Road was easy enough, but to locate the gypsies' encampment was another matter.

"They may have pitched their tents along any one of these side roads," Nancy commented. "It's so dark and wooded, we probably couldn't see the spot unless we were right on top of it."

"Looks like a bad storm coming, too," Ned said, rolling the window up part way. "That'll make it harder to find the place."

Suddenly a flash of lightning cut across the inky sky, revealing a mass of ugly, boiling clouds.

"Maybe we'd better postpone our search and start for home," Nancy suggested.

Ned agreed, and turned the car in the narrow road. Before they had travelled two miles, the storm broke. During the slow drive back the rain came down in torrents, and it was not until they reached River Heights that it stopped.

"Lucky we started back when we did," Nancy said as she bade Ned good night at her own door-step. "Hope your boys' camp wasn't washed out!"

"If it was, I'll be ready for another date with you in the morning," he laughed.

Early the next day, George and Bess came to the Drew home to ask Nancy what progress had been made on repairing the sailboat. She told them Sam Pickard was working as fast as he could, but still would not promise to finish the job in time for the yacht-club races.

"I was hoping the boat would be ready so we could take her for a trial run this morning," George grumbled. "Another day wasted!"

"Not for me," replied Nancy. "I'm starting off to find some missing gypsies. How about coming along?"

George was all for the adventure, but cautious Bess reminded them of their unpleasant experience some days before at the camp on the river.

"You two must like being thrown out by gypsies!" she remarked.

Nevertheless, Bess decided to go along, and up to the time they reached Winchester, was very gay, chatting about a new tearoom she had found in River Heights, to the detriment of her figure. But as they turned up a side road on the far side of the town, and learned from a passing farmer exactly where the gypsies were, she began to grow uneasy.

When the three girls finally reached the wooded spot, though, she sighed in relief. There was no one in sight. The tribe had departed, leaving only the charred remains of their fires.

"Maybe Murko will show up at the broadcasting studio sometime today," George suggested, noting Nancy's keen disappointment.

"I doubt it, but we'll stop there," Nancy replied, heading the car back towards Winchester.

A few minutes later they reached the radio station, and were told by the manager that "Mr Martin" would broadcast no more. A gypsy woman had come there early that morning and left a note from the violinist. The message had merely said he would never again play over that station.

"We had a contract with him, too," the manager said, "but still there's nothing we can do about it."

Nancy and the other girls were about to leave, when he called, "Are you Miss Nancy Drew?" To her "Yes," he added, "There's something here for you. It was brought by that gypsy woman who left the note. She merely said to give it to Miss Nancy Drew."

From an inner office the man brought out a package. Puzzled, Nancy decided to open it at once. Inside was a red, black and white hand-woven blanket.

"This is strange," she remarked. "Did the woman leave her name?"

"No, I scarcely noticed her, except that she had blue eyes unlike most gypsies, and was about fifty years old."

Nancy caught up a corner of the blanket. In small letters was woven a name—*H. Bostwick*.

"Could it be Henrietta Bostwick?" she wondered,

remembering the name on the album she had bought in New York. "If so, is she a gypsy? Or does she merely live with the tribe? And why did she send me this blanket?"

On the way home Nancy discussed the incident with Bess and George. "I feel sure that that woman was trying to send me some information," she concluded.

Upon returning to her own home, she seated herself on the living room floor and examined every inch of the gypsy blanket.

"These figures sprawled here and there mean something, I'm sure of it!" she told herself. "If only I could get at the crux of the thing, I might have a valuable clue!"

An outside door slammed. Hannah, packages in her arms, came into the room.

"Shopping is an awful trial these . . ." she began, then interrupted herself to exclaim, "Nancy! Where did you get that!"

"It's a gift from a gypsy."

"Destroy it! Get it out of the house!" Hannah cried.

"Why, what's wrong?" the girl asked, amazed.

"Look at the letters on it!"

"Letters?"

"They spell 'Beware!' " Hannah pointed to a blotch of red figures.

From where Nancy was sitting the word became a part of the pattern and could not be made out. Jumping up, the girl darted to the housekeeper's side.

"Why, it does!" she agreed. "Hannah, you darling! You're helping me solve this mystery!"

Greatly excited, Nancy began to twist and turn the blanket, trying to find other words hidden in the maze of geometrical figures.

"Hannah, do you see anything else?" she asked eagerly.

Mrs Gruen shook her head. She and Nancy walked into the hall to study the blanket from a distance. Suddenly Nancy exclaimed:

"I have it! I see it!" She gave the housekeeper an excited hug.

"What is it?" Mrs Gruen asked.

Nancy gook a quick step forward and pointed out three more words—*king and sun.*

"It says, '*Beware King and Sun!*'"

"Yes, it does," the woman agreed, "but I don't see any sense in those words."

"There must be a meaning to it all! The word 'king' could refer to Zorus, the gypsy chief! I can't figure out 'sun'. The message might mean, '*Beware of the King and his Son!*'"

"You always did have a lively imagination," said Mrs Gruen.

Nancy scarcely heard her. Thinking aloud, she continued, "If the word is 'son', who could he be? Anton, perhaps, or maybe Romano, Rose's father?"

"The word isn't 'son'," Hannah insisted. "It says 'sun', plain as day. Are gypsies sun worshippers?"

Nancy's eyes opened wide! Without answering the housekeeper's question, she exclaimed:

"Why didn't I think of it before! 'Sun' is the word and it means 'source of light'! *Beware the King and his source of light!*

"Well, at long last, light is beginning to dawn on *me*!"

• 19 • *The Mannequin's Hint*

NANCY rushed to the telephone and called state police headquarters. After identifying herself as Carson Drew's daughter, she said, "Will you please try to locate the gypsy tribe that moved out of Winchester recently? And when you do, will someone from your office go there with me?"

The officer listened carefully as she gave a brief resumé of all the things that had happened in which she thought certain gypsies had been involved, saying she thought the guilty ones might be hiding in that particular tribe.

"We'll start working at once and let you know what we find out," the man promised.

While waiting to hear from him, Nancy dashed over to Mrs Struthers' home to show her the strange blanket. Rose was having a music lesson and Nancy could hear the clear, true notes of a violin. She thought the teacher must be playing, but Mrs Struthers smiled proudly, saying:

"That's Rose. Isn't she doing well? And her dancing is remarkable. Oh, Nancy, she's so happy now and I have you to thank for everything. If we only could find her father and the mysterious doll . . ."

"I have a new idea," said Nancy. "It came to me after looking at this gift from some strange gypsy woman."

Mrs Struthers gazed in awe at the blanket and felt sure it carried an unfriendly warning. But Nancy did not share her anxiety.

"I have a new theory I want to work on," she said, "but to start on it I'd like a little more information about

117

your daughter's illness. Would you mind if I ask the doctor about it?"

"No, indeed. He was Dr Tiffen. I'm sure he'll talk with you, although he always says Enid's illness was a puzzle to him."

Nancy went to Dr Tiffen's office, where she learned that the illness was not so much of a puzzle as he had pretended to Mrs Struthers and her daughter.

"I did not think it wise to tell them. I knew Enid could not live long," the doctor revealed. "What did puzzle me, though, was why at times she seemed to have abundant energy, and at others she had almost none."

"You gave her medicine?" Nancy asked.

"Oh, yes, but that was to ease her pain. In cases such as hers, I know of nothing to prescribe to give a patient energy."

"Dr Tiffen," Nancy said, smiling up at him, "I have a theory which may be crazy, but if you have time, may I tell you what it is?"

"Every once in a while a layman hits on an idea which is a great boon to mankind," he smiled back. Then, after hearing how Nancy had figured out that "source of light" meant the sun, and since from the sun comes energy, possibly through some secret known to Rose's mother, she had received momentary energy, he added, "You may be right."

"If you think there's something to my theory, I'm going to try to find that 'source of light,' " the girl declared.

Before she got to her car, Dr Tiffen called her back saying she was wanted on the telephone. Mrs Struthers was calling to tell Nancy that the police had just notified her that they had found part of her stolen property in a Winchester pawnshop.

"They're holding several suspects and one of them may be that pick-pocket who stole my jewelled bag. He may also be the one who robbed the house. Could you go over to Winchester, Nancy dear, and identify him?"

The girl glanced at her wrist watch. She could just about make it there and back before dark, and thus keep her promise to her father and Hannah that she would not be out alone at night while working on the Struthers case.

"I'll run right over," she agreed.

For the second time that day Nancy headed her car for Winchester. Should any of the men in the police line-up be those she suspected as thieves, she hoped that they would confess and by so doing clear up a large part of the mystery. But unfortunately she had never seen any of them before.

Leaving the police station, Nancy realised suddenly that she was dreadfully hungry. She bought a glass of milk to cut her appetite, then hurried to River Heights for a belated but delicious dinner.

Early the next morning she received a call from a state police officer.

"Miss Drew," he said, "we've found that gypsy tribe. They're on the south side of Hancock. One of the men from the station near there will go with you. What time can you reach Hancock?"

"About nine-thirty. Thank you very much."

As soon as Nancy and the housekeeper had had breakfast, the girl went off, her hopes high. Now perhaps she would find Romano Pepito! If not, surely she would pick up a clue to the whereabouts of Anton, Nitaka, and perhaps even Murko. He might tell her who left the blanket with the strange message.

At exactly nine-thirty Nancy walked into the Hancock police station. A uniformed policeman was assigned to accompany her to the gypsy settlement. As they approached the secluded place, they were greeted by barking dogs.

The warning sent members of the tribe scurrying towards their tents. Women, who had been cooking meat over cherry-red fires, hastily gathered their playing children and retreated. When the officer addressed a question to a young woman who scurried past, she replied, "Ci janav." He explained to Nancy this meant, "I don't know."

The same reply was received from other fleeing figures. Evidently the gypsies had no intention of giving any information to the police!

One man did come forward, making a pretence of welcoming the couple. He announced himself as the leader of the tribe. Nancy had never seen him before, nor any of the gypsies who were peering curiously from the door-ways of their tents. So far as she could judge, this was not the tribe she had visited on the river.

Politely, she asked if Zorus, Murko, Romano Pepito, Anton, Nitaka, Tony Wassell or Henrietta Bostwick were there. The leader shook his head at the mention of each name.

"The persons I'm looking for aren't here," she said, turning to the policeman.

"Just the same, we'll make sure and not take anyone's word for it," replied the officer.

He did some investigating on his own account, but came back convinced that the pick-pocket was not hiding in the camp.

"If he was here, he fled before we came," the officer decided.

Before getting into the car, Nancy bought a string of beads from a young woman. Then she and the policeman left.

Nancy got back to River Heights just as the clock in the town-hall tower chimed the midday hour. She loved to listen to it and often laughingly told Hannah Gruen that it made her feel as though the old bell were announcing the end of one adventure and the beginning of another.

"For me it means nothing more mysterious than a lunch date with Bess and George, and a look at the mannequin dolls' wedding party," she reflected with a chuckle.

At one o'clock she met the cousins at the new tearoom Bess had recommended.

"Let's walk to Taylor's from here," Bess suggested after they finished a hearty meal. "I feel ten pounds heavier."

The department store was fairly near. George told her cousin she should walk up the five flights to the doll exhibit as well, if she expected to lose weight. Bess grimaced and got in the lift.

The showroom was already crowded when the girls entered, but they managed to make their way to the front and were thrilled at the exquisite scene on the stage. Six dainty bridesmaids stood in attendance on a beautiful bride.

"Did you ever see anything so lovely?" whispered Bess. "Especially the bride! She looks real enough to walk right down the aisle!"

Nancy gazed fixedly at the mannequin bride, and her thoughts started to rove far afield. She recalled the gypsy wedding at the carnival, and how the child bride had received a symbolic doll as part of the ceremony. Then she thought of the photograph Mrs Struthers had shown her of Rose's mother in her white bridal gown.

"Girls!" she whispered excitedly. "We must go at once to Mrs Struthers'! I believe I have it . . . the answer to the mystery! It's in the old album after all!"

· 20 · *A Detective Fails*

BESS AND GEORGE were startled by Nancy's sudden declaration.

"In *which* old album?" asked George excitedly. "You've uncovered so many that I can hardly keep track of them all."

Nancy grinned at her friend. "It's not that confusing, George," she said. "I'm sure we can find the clue in that old album of Mrs Struthers'."

"The one the precious stones were stolen from?" exclaimed Bess.

"Right!" returned Nancy. "Let's hurry over to her house and I'll show you what I mean."

The three girls soon reached the Struthers' home and hurried inside. While the others watched in bewilderment, Nancy quickly flipped through the pages of the brass filigree album until she came to the photograph of Enid Struthers in her bridal gown.

"Do you notice anything odd about this picture?" she inquired excitedly.

In turn, George, Bess and Mrs Struthers examined the photograph and shook their heads.

"Don't you see anything unnatural about it?" persisted Nancy.

Rose, who had joined the group, volunteered her opinion. "It looks more like a doll than it does my mummy!"

"Exactly!" cried Nancy, pleased to have her hunch

confirmed. "Rose, I'm sure that this isn't a photograph of your mother. It's a picture of a doll made to look like her!"

"Why, Nancy, that's fantastic!" exclaimed Mrs Struthers. "This *is* my daughter!"

"If you'll look closely at the face, you can see an artificiality about it," Nancy declared.

The others scrutinised the picture carefully, and realised that Nancy was right.

"Such a lifelike doll makes those mannequins at Taylor's look like sticks," remarked George.

"But seeing them gave me the idea about this picture," Nancy smiled.

"How do you account for the doll being made?" asked Mrs Struthers.

"My guess is that Romano, being a gypsy, wanted to follow their custom of presenting a doll to his bride. Since she was not a child and not a gypsy, he had one made to look like her in her bridal dress. He probably thought it so attractive that he had it photographed."

"But why go to all that trouble?" asked George. "Why didn't he just take a picture of Mrs Pepito herself?"

"If I had the answer to that," replied Nancy, "I'd have the key to the whole mystery." To herself she said, "Maybe Enid didn't have a bridal dress of her own."

"What do you suppose became of the doll?" Mrs Struthers asked. "If Enid had it, why didn't she show it to me or to Rose?"

"Perhaps your daughter was forced to sell the doll," Nancy speculated. "Or possibly her husband took it with him."

"Without doubt this doll in the picture is the one I'm to find for Rose," said Mrs Struthers. "But what importance could it have for her? During the last few days of Enid's life, she did say she had expected Rose to be well off financially, some day, but that the hope had been lost.

Could that have had some connection with the doll itself?"

Instead of answering, Nancy looked at the elderly woman and asked, "Mrs Struthers, at the time of your daughter's illness, did you have the same servants you have now?"

"No, a Mrs Hunt was with us then. She was our house-keeper and very attentive to Enid."

"Where is Mrs Hunt now?"

"She has retired to a little cottage near the edge of River Heights. It was through her that I came here. Do you think that she might know something helpful which she did not tell me?"

"Possibly," replied Nancy.

"Then do call on her," said Mrs Struthers.

As the girls left the house, George and Bess suddenly remembered that they had promised to meet their mothers in town to go shopping. Nancy dropped them off and drove to the former housekeeper's home alone.

Mrs Hunt was rather reserved at first, but Nancy's straightforward and sincere manner impressed her, and when the woman seemed satisfied that Nancy wanted to help Rose and her grandmother, she willingly told her everything she knew about Enid Struthers.

"I felt so sorry for the poor girl," she murmured. "Her marriage to Romano Pepito brought her happiness for only a short time. She didn't confide in her mother about her fears, but she did tell me a few things."

"Did she ever mention a doll made to look like her?" Nancy asked eagerly.

"No, she didn't. If she had one, she probably kept it in a small trunk in her room."

Nancy looked surprised, for Mrs Struthers had never mentioned the trunk to her.

"Enid always wore the key to it on a ribbon around her neck," Mrs Hunt added. "She never opened the trunk when anyone was near."

"What became of it?"

"Mrs Struthers may still have it. I don't know. But the contents are gone now. They were removed by Enid before she died."

"Do you know why?"

"About a week before poor Enid passed away, she and I were alone in the house. A woman came to see her. They talked for a long while together. Then they went to Enid's bedroom."

"Did Mrs Pepito seem upset?"

"No, she seemed very pleased about the whole affair. The visitor finally left, carrying a rather large package. After that, Enid never bothered to lock the trunk, and one day when it was open, I noticed it was empty."

"You've no idea what it was she gave away?"

"Not the slightest. For a day or two she was very happy, telling me her broken life was about to be set right. Then seemingly for no reason she became discouraged and began to cry a good deal. Her illness, which I believe was an incurable one, intensified, and she passed away rather suddenly."

"She said nothing about her visitor?"

"Not directly, but when I mentioned her, Enid said please not to tell her mother anyone had been there."

"Mrs Struthers told me that Enid on her deathbed begged her mother to find a certain doll. She seemed to want it for Rose."

"Yes," Mrs Hunt nodded sadly, "but we couldn't figure out what she meant."

"Do you recall what the woman who came after the package looked like?" Nancy asked.

"Yes, indeed. She was of medium height and well dressed. Her eyes were dark and piercing . . . the kind that usually go with coal-black hair. But her hair I guess was bleached. Anyway, it was a strange shade . . . a kind of carrot colour."

"Oh!" cried Nancy. "I believe I know who she was!"

"You do?" asked Mrs Hunt, astounded.

Nancy did not say that she thought the caller had been Nitaka, but she felt sure of it. Oh, the pieces of the puzzle were beginning to fall into place rapidly now!

"I'm glad you called," Mrs Hunt declared as the girl announced she must leave. "You're a true friend of Mrs Struthers and I can see you want to help her."

"I hope I can."

"Well, I don't mean to discourage you, my dear, but that detective she hired never was able to learn anything about the doll. Nor was he able to trace the woman who called on Enid, when I told him about her."

"Mrs Struthers hired a detective?"

"Immediately after her daughter passed away. He charged her an enormous price, in return for doing absolutely nothing!"

"I hope *I* shan't fail," Nancy said with determination. "By the way, part of my work is to find Rose's father. Mrs Struthers believes the family should be reunited."

Mrs Hunt was amazed to hear this, but delighted as well.

"At first I was looking for Romano Pepito to find out about the doll," Nancy explained. "Then I came across a picture of him and showed it to Rose and her grandmother." She smiled. "He's handsome and kind looking. Now they want to have him join the family!"

Mrs Hunt smiled too. "I'm so glad. Enid was deeply in love with her husband, and I'm sure he must be a fine man. By the way, how is Rose? She was rather unmanageable during her mother's illness."

Nancy reported the improvement in Rose's behaviour and mentioned her musical talent. "I believe that she'll be on the concert stage and in films one of these days," she prophesied.

"Oh, I'm so pleased," Mrs Hunt said, as she opened the door for her caller and bade her goodbye.

On the way home Nancy suddenly remembered that she

had promised Hannah Gruen to make a trip out to the farm where the housekeeper bought chickens each week.

"I'll do it now," she decided, and turned into the country.

Her purchase made, the girl started down the steep, high-banked lane from the farmhouse. At the junction with the main road she came to a dead stop to look for passing cars. A car whizzed by at high speed, but not too fast for Nancy to catch a glimpse of the driver's face.

"The pick-pocket!" she exclaimed, hardly daring to believe her eyes. "*In a black saloon!*"

There were no other cars on the road, so she quickly turned into the main road and pursued the man's black saloon. As she pulled nearer, he must have realised that Nancy was trying to overtake him, for he put on a burst of speed. Nancy did the same.

The chase was on!

• 21 •   *The Television Clue*

NANCY became aware of a roaring noise behind her. A second later a motorcycle policeman drew up alongside and motioned to her to pull over.

"You know how fast you're going?" he bawled. "We've got laws, you know!"

Nancy slowed down but did not stop. Pointing to the car ahead, which was disappearing from view, she cried:

"That driver . . . he's a thief! Please go after him! I'll follow and explain."

The policeman, not sure but that this might be a way of getting rid of him, said, "Who are you?"

"Nancy Drew. Carson Drew's daugh . . ."

The officer waited for no more. Like a released rocket he shot down the road. Nancy, following at top speed, presently saw him overtake the saloon. It pulled to the side of the road, and the driver handed the policeman something through the open window.

"Probably his licence," the girl surmised.

As Nancy reached them and looked the driver square in the face, she knew without a doubt he was the pick-pocket.

"Mr Rosser here says he's innocent of your charge," the policeman said to Nancy.

"Rosser? Why, his name is Tony Wassell," Nancy told the policeman.

"Officer, you see from my licence what my name is," the man declared indignantly. "I've never seen this girl before and I don't know what she's talking about. Now, if you're through with me, I'll go along."

"Not so fast," the officer said. "Tony Wassell, eh? That name's in the police records."

"Yes," Nancy spoke up, "he's the man who stole a handbag with money and other valuables from Mrs John Struthers."

"Oh, so you're the guy," said the officer, remembering the case. "And if you're Tony Wassell, you're the gypsy we've got other charges against."

"I'm not a gypsy!" the man retorted angrily.

"Wait until Anton and Nitaka hear about this!" Nancy said, hoping to trap him into betraying an association with the couple.

"Anton and Nitaka!" The man spoke the words involuntarily, a look of dismay crossing his face.

"You three work for the king, don't you?" Nancy quizzed him.

The gypsy's eyes blazed. "What do you know about the king?" he demanded.

"More than you think!" the girl replied. "And you were

so afraid I'd have you arrested, you sent me a warning note and then tried to shove my car off the road and injure me so I couldn't work on the Struthers case. And when I reported you to the police, you put a hole in my boat, just for revenge."

The gypsy, still protesting his innocence, was taken to police headquarters for further questioning. There he stubbornly maintained a stony silence. The only time he spoke was when one of the officers asked him if he wanted a lawyer, or would like to get in touch with anyone he knew.

"No!" the thief snapped. "Leave me alone!"

Nancy took Mrs Struthers to the police station the next morning to prefer charges against him. Even then the prisoner refused to admit anything or tell what he had done with the contents of the woman's bag.

"He'll talk after he's been here a few days," an officer told Nancy knowingly.

When she returned home a little later, she found Ned Nickerson on the porch swing eating some biscuits Hannah had just baked. He listened attentively to Nancy's vivid account of the pick-pocket's capture, and then observed:

"Nice going, Nancy, but how about doing a little playing just for a change? One crook in jail is enough for any detective! I have two days off."

Nancy smiled. "Fine idea! Let's have a picnic on the river on Monday if it's clear. And while I'm down there, I can take care of something."

"Not sleuthing?" groaned Ned.

"No, so relax," she laughed. "I want to stop at Mr Pickard's to see how he's getting along with *Whip the Wind*."

"That's different," Ned said.

When he arrived at eleven o'clock on Monday morning, Nancy handed him a tempting-looking lunch hamper.

"How about a couple of Dad's fishing rods? Shall we take them?" she asked.

"Great idea. I'll get them."

Fifteen minutes later Nancy and Ned were on their way. While he went off to buy bait, she stepped into the boat repair shop. Sam Pickard was hard at work. The damaged plank had been removed from *Whip the Wind*, and the old man was planing down another to fit in its place.

"How's the work going?" Nancy asked brightly.

"Not so good," Mr Pickard complained.

"Can't you hurry things a little?" Nancy asked him.

"Ain't promisin'," the old man replied. "Told you that when I took the job."

"Yes, you did," Nancy agreed. "Well, I know you'll do the best you can."

Not far from Pickard's there were motorboats for hire. Ned selected one, and soon the couple were heading downstream.

"Where to?" he asked.

"Dad says there's good fishing in Pilot's Cove," Nancy replied.

Ned turned the boat in that direction and by the time they had reached the spot, they were both ready for the generous lunch Hannah had packed. They fished during the afternoon, and enjoyed competing with each other. When they finally reeled in their lines, Ned had five fish and Nancy three.

"What'll we do with all these fish?" Nancy laughed, as Ned started the motorboat.

"We might call on the Wyatts," he suggested. "They have a cottage not far from here."

"You mean Hazel and Bill?" Nancy asked, referring to a young engineer and his wife who had been married only a short time.

"Yes. We'll bring the fish and stay to dinner," Ned joked.

"I'd love to see them," Nancy grinned.

Ned headed for the channel of the Muskoka River. Four miles south, they tied up in front of a small, picturesque stone house perched on a hillside overlooking the water. To their delight, they found the Wyatts at home.

"Well, it's about time you came to see us!" Hazel cried, greeting them enthusiastically. "You're staying to dinner, too. No excuses!"

"Thanks, we will," Ned accepted without consulting Nancy. "And here's part of our meal," he added, presenting Hazel with the fish.

For an hour the young people sat on the stone terrace, chatting and sipping frosty cool drinks. Bill spoke of his interesting work in the manufacture of television equipment and said:

"I want you to see our set. It's the last word in television."

"Any good programmes on now?" Hazel asked. "This time is usually given over to children's stories, and adult programmes come on later."

Bill scanned a schedule he had brought home from the studio. Finally he said:

"Sudden change of programme here. There's to be a Thomas Smith on at eight o'clock. Someone at the studio says he's good. Plays the violin. He's never been televised, and unless someone tells him, he won't even know about it. The new equipment we installed is marvellous."

Nancy was interested at once. "Let's tune in to that programme," she suggested.

A little before eight Bill turned on the set. Nancy and Ned marvelled at the clearness of the colours on the screen and the quality of the sound reproduction. When the next programme came on, an announcer introduced Thomas Smith. The artist walked to the centre of the stage and put his violin under his chin. He had played only the first few notes of the *Gypsy Love Song*, when Nancy cried out:

"Romano Pepito!"

"You know him?" exclaimed Hazel Wyatt in surprise.

"Only from his picture," Nancy answered. "I've been trying to find him. It's terribly important that I talk to him. If I were only at that studio right now!"

Bill jumped up. "I'll call the station and ask that the man be kept there until you can drive over," he offered. "Take our car."

Nancy and Ned waited only long enough to make sure the station manager knew they were en route to meet the violinist. Then, with a forty-mile drive ahead of them, they set off for the town of Aiken. Two detours and a delay at a bridge made the trip longer than they anticipated.

"It's taken us almost an hour!" Nancy said as they alighted in front of the broadcasting company offices. "Oh, Ned, I hope Romano is still here. It will be the best break I've had yet!"

• 22 •   Double Disappearance

NANCY AND NED were whisked up in the lift to the third floor of the radio station. Anxiously they inquired for the violinist. Daniel Brownell, the manager, came to speak to them.

"I'm very sorry we could not keep Thomas Smith here," he said regretfully. "We tried our best, but he insisted upon leaving."

"You told him it was very important?" Nancy asked, her heart sinking.

Mr Brownell nodded. "The only way we could have kept

him was by force. Naturally we couldn't do that. He left about forty-five minutes ago."

"I must see him," Nancy told the man. "Can you tell me where he went?"

"Sorry, I haven't the slightest idea. And I'm afraid he won't be back."

"Why?" Ned asked.

"Smith was furious when he found we'd televised his programme," Mr Brownell answered. "He's a temperamental fellow. When Smith came here, he said he didn't want to meet anyone. Acted strangely, as if he were afraid of somebody."

Nancy briefly explained to the manager that it was of great importance to the violinist that she contact him. "Surely you have his home address?" she asked.

"Well, it's most unusual for us to give out such information."

"My father, Carson Drew, will vouch for me," Nancy pleaded. "Finding Mr Smith may mean a great deal to his future happiness."

Apparently Mr Brownell had heard of Carson Drew, or Nancy's sincerity convinced him of her desire to help Smith, for he stepped into an office, returning a moment later. In his hand was a slip of paper with Thomas Smith's address. Thanking him, Nancy and Ned drove directly to the place. It was a boarding house in a poor section of the city.

"I have a feeling he won't be here," Nancy predicted as they climbed the steps.

Her hunch that Romano had fled was correct. They learned that the man known as Thomas Smith had taken all his belongings and departed hastily.

"He just left?" Nancy questioned the landlady.

"Not ten minutes ago."

"Did he say where he was going?"

"No. I asked him if he wanted his fan mail forwarded

and he answered, 'The only mail I want can never come.'
Then he jumped into an Acme taxi and drove off."

Nancy and Ned walked to the car. Realising that they
had to return the hired motorboat and were using a
borrowed car, Ned felt it would be best to abandon a
further search for Mr Smith for the time being.

"We'd better go back to the Wyatts," he said.

Reluctantly Nancy nodded assent. She felt frustrated,
coming so close to finding Romano, only to fail.

"He may have gone to one of the nearby gypsy camps,"
she said, giving voice to her thoughts. "I'll come back here
tomorrow and see if I can pick up his trail."

"You never give up, do you?" Ned asked. "That's one
of the things I like about you, Nancy."

It was late before the young people reached River
Heights. Nancy slept soundly but was up early the next
morning, eager to get on the trail of Romano Pepito. She
thought of calling the Struthers home to tell them the
latest developments but decided against this.

"No use disappointing them if nothing comes of my hunt,"
she told Hannah Gruen.

"You're not going alone?" the housekeeper asked,
worried.

"Not if Bess and George will go with me."

After breakfast, she telephoned the girls to ask them if
they would accompany her to Aiken.

"Sure thing," said George, and Bess echoed the senti-
ment.

By midday they were in the small town of Aiken, ready
to take up the search for the missing violinist.

"I'm terribly hungry," Bess observed. "Let's eat before
we start hunting for that violinist."

"First, let's go to the Acme Taxi Company and see what
we can find out," Nancy suggested. "It was one of their
men who drove Romano from his boarding house."

"I hope he'll remember where he took his passenger,"

said George, as they parked the car in front of the Acme office.

Nancy, finding the manager, asked if he would mind answering a few questions.

"It's okay with me," he said genially.

"Did any of your drivers happen to mention calling for a man with a violin, at a boarding house on the west side of town last night?"

"Might have been Gus Frankey. He answered a call from over there. Say, did Gus report in this morning?" he asked, turning to an assistant at a nearby desk.

"Didn't show up," the other replied. "We've phoned his house six times. Wife's wild—says he didn't come home last night."

"Did he turn in his cab?"

"No."

"He must have taken a passenger on a long trip." The manager turned again to Nancy. "Gus probably is the driver you want to see."

"While we're waiting for him, we may as well find a place to eat," Bess insisted impatiently. "I'm starved!"

"You said that before," grinned George. "Oh, well, I guess Nancy and I will have to bow to that big appetite of yours. But I thought you were going on a diet!"

As the girls walked down the street looking for a tearoom, Nancy suddenly stopped.

"One of Mrs Struthers' stolen dolls!" she exclaimed, pointing towards the window of an attractive shop.

Amid a display of fine old porcelain figures stood the dainty little lady on a velvet box, holding her fan and bouquet. Quickly Nancy entered the shop. A pleasant elderly woman came forward. At Nancy's request she took the doll from the window.

"Normally I handle only porcelain figurines," she explained, "but when this doll was offered to me, I couldn't resist her."

"Would you mind telling me from whom you bought it?" Nancy asked. "The doll is really a collector's piece, isn't it?"

"Indeed it is. The woman who sold it said she had bought it in Paris. She's disposing of her collection."

"Did the woman by chance have olive skin and carrot-coloured hair?" Nancy asked.

"Yes, she did," the shop owner replied.

"Then I'm afraid you were sold a stolen doll by a gypsy named Nitaka," Nancy said, sorry to have to reveal such unpleasant news. "When did you buy it?"

"Only yesterday."

Nancy turned to Bess and George. "That might mean Anton and Nitaka are somewhere near here, as well as Romano!" she exclaimed.

The shopkeeper was confused by the girl's reference to persons whom she did not know. "It never occurred to me that the doll was stolen," she said nervously.

Nancy was looking about for a telephone. "I think we'd better call the owner of the doll," she said.

"I hope she won't blame me for buying it," said the shopkeeper.

"I'm sure she won't," Nancy assured her. "Mrs Struthers is very kind. I'll explain everything to her."

Bess spoke up. "You'll probably be hours on the phone, Nancy. Suppose George and I go to find something to eat. We'll get sandwiches and bring them back to the car."

"All right," said Nancy, and picked up the telephone.

She placed the call, and presently heard Mrs Struthers' voice on the line. Instantly she knew from the tone of it that something had gone wrong. Before she could mention having found the stolen doll, Mrs Struthers cried:

"Oh, Nancy, the most dreadful thing has happened! I've been trying to get hold of you. Rose has disappeared! We're afraid she may have been kidnapped."

"How terrible!" exclaimed Nancy. "When did this happen?"

"Just this morning. Oh, what'll I do? What'll I do?"

"Maybe she only went to visit one of her playmates' houses," Nancy suggested, trying to soothe the woman.

"No, we've looked everywhere."

"Did you call the police?"

"Yes, everyone is searching for her, but no one's seen her since she went out to play in the garden this morning. Oh, I'm desperate. If anything should happen to that child . . ."

"Mrs Struthers, it's just possible Rose ran away of her own accord," Nancy suggested quickly.

"Why would she do that?"

"Rose has talked a good bit lately about going into radio and films," said Nancy. "She may have taken a train to New York to try for an audition."

"Oh, Nancy, you may be right. Her violin is gone too."

Actually Nancy did not think this was what had happened. Rather, she felt that Mrs Struthers' first guess was correct; that Rose had been kidnapped. After promising Mrs Struthers she would do everything possible to find her granddaughter, Nancy was in a quandary. Should she go back to River Heights or keep on trying to find Romano? It was just possible, she decided, *there might be a connection between the two disappearances!*

Turning from the telephone, she arranged with the owner of the shop to keep the doll until some arrangement could be made for Mrs Struthers to claim it. Then Nancy hurried back to the Acme Taxi Company.

As she arrived, a cab, dusty as if from a long trip, turned into the garage. The girl wondered if this could be the one that Thomas Smith had hired. Impulsively she stopped the driver to inquire if he were Gus Frankey and, hearing he was, asked if he had picked up a violinist by the name of Thomas Smith at the studio the night before.

"I sure did," the man answered. "Worse luck for me!"

"What do you mean?"

"I'd rather not say."

"It's important that I find Mr Smith," Nancy said urgently. "Where is he?"

"You'd need a map to find the place."

Nancy wondered why the man was so evasive. It was maddening when time was fleeting. Rose had disappeared, and Romano might be within reach!

"Listen," said Nancy, "this may be a life-and-death matter. If you don't think I can find the place where you taxied Mr Smith, you'll have to take me there yourself!"

"Hold on, miss. I can't go back there now. I've been out all night."

"You wouldn't want to be responsible for harm coming to an innocent person . . ."

The man's eyes opened wide. " 'Course not. Just the same, I won't go unless the company manager gives his okay. I've got reasons . . ."

Nancy called the manager from the office.

"This girl wants me to make another long trip," the cab driver complained to his superior. "I've been out all night and had a tough time."

"It's vital that I find the passenger this man carried last night," Nancy interposed excitedly. "I'll pay well for the trip. But please hurry."

"Take her, Gus," the manager ordered. "You can have time off later."

As Gus went unwillingly to fill up his taxi with petrol and telephone his wife, Nancy glanced anxiously down the street for Bess and George. They were not in sight. Telling Gus she would be right back, the girl jumped into her own car and quickly drove through several streets in the town. The cousins were nowhere in view.

"I can't wait for them much longer," she decided, "or Gus will change his mind."

Reaching the garage, she found the girls still had not returned. The taxi driver was fuming.

"If you don't go now," he said, "I'm going home to bed, boss or no boss."

"All right."

Quickly she wrote her friends a note of explanation and left it on the front seat of her car. Then, having asked the manager to keep his eye on the car until the girls came, she hopped into Gus's taxi and was driven away.

"By the way, how far are we going?" she asked as they turned into the country. "And where?"

"To that gypsy camp on the mountain south of Aiken," he replied. "And, believe me, if the boss hadn't ordered me to do this, you wouldn't get me near that place with a ten-foot pole! I had the scare of my life there!"

• 23 •   *An Unexpected Reunion*

NANCY was thunderstruck at the taxi-driver's words. He had been to a gypsy camp and had had a bad scare! Maybe she herself was running into danger going to the place!

"You took Mr Smith to a gypsy camp?"

"Sure, and spent the whole night, there, too," the cab driver replied. "When I arrived, a couple of men rushed out and took me inside. There was some kind of feast and they gave me a lot to eat and drink. Then I tried to leave, but they wouldn't let me. I must see some dancing, they said, then eat some more."

"But what scared you?" Nancy prompted.

"The fortune-teller. She told me awful things."

"You didn't believe her?"

"I did last night. Maybe she was wrong, though," the driver admitted. "But I haven't told you the worst part. I can't prove it, but I'll bet they drugged me. I must have gone to sleep while the fortune-teller was talking. The next thing I knew I woke up in my own cab this morning. What I can't figure out, is why they did it."

Nancy thought she could. The gypsies were expecting Rose to be brought there! Since the time of the girl's arrival was somewhat uncertain, they had decided to hold Gus until they were sure he would not find out what was going on and report the incident to the Aiken police!

"What became of Mr Smith?" Nancy asked.

"Dunno," the driver answered. "Never saw him again."

By this time the taxi had reached a seldom used track which led to the mountain. Presently the cab drew up at the entrance to a lane.

"This is as far as I'm going," announced the driver. "You're on your own from here."

"But . . ."

"Now don't give me any trouble," Gus said grimly. "I'm not setting foot in that camp again!"

"Then wait for me here."

"I'm not waiting either. You couldn't pay me enough to keep me here. I'm going home!"

Thoroughly annoyed by the man's lack of co-operation, Nancy was tempted to tell him why she had come. Before she made up her mind, he said:

"You owe me three dollars and twenty-five cents. I got to get goin'."

"I may need your help," Nancy told him.

"Say, what is this anyway? I didn't want to come here in the first place. If you're afraid to go inside alone, then jump in the cab and I'll drive you back to Aiken."

"No" Nancy decided. "I'll go alone. But please do me

one favour," she pleaded as she handed Gus the fare and a generous tip. "Telephone my home in River Heights and ask that my father come here at once if he can. And if you see my two friends at your garage or on the road in my car, please tell them, too. Be sure to give them explicit directions, because I don't want to be stranded here."

"Sure, I'll do that much for you, miss. Only don't ask me to come back here. Give me your father's telephone number."

Nancy scribbled it on the back of an old envelope in her bag. After the taxi pulled away, she walked rapidly towards the gypsy camp, which was screened from view by trees.

Finally she left the lane and walked among the trees to avoid detection. She could see gypsies moving about, but so far her approach to the settlement apparently had not been noticed.

Suddenly a tall, handsome man with a red sash about his waist crossed the clearing. Tucked under his arm was a violin.

Romano Pepito! At last she had found him!

As he entered one of the tents, Nancy's heart beat wildly. "This is my chance!" she thought.

The girl was wondering how to slip into the tent without attracting notice, when at the other end of the camp she heard sounds of laughing, excited children. A group, which included several adults, was marching forward. From her hiding place Nancy fastened her eyes upon a girl in gay gypsy dress who was the centre of attention.

"It's Rose!" she gasped as they came closer. "The gypsies did bring her here!"

Much to Nancy's surprise, Rose did not look worried or frightened; instead, she seemed happy in her new surroundings. Grabbing a tambourine from one of the women, the girl started to dance.

"There!" she cried breathlessly, as the exhibition ended. "I can dance as well as any gypsy!"

A fat old woman in a scarlet skirt took Rose by the hand, leading her to a tent which had the symbol of the sun above the canvas doorway.

"You will stay here until Zorus tells you what to do," she told the girl.

In her fear of what might happen to Rose, Nancy forgot her desire to talk to Romano. Instead, she waited until the group had scattered. Then, when no one was near by, she slipped inside the tent.

"Nancy!" Rose cried.

"Sh! I have only a moment to talk, and you must listen closely!"

"I'm not going back home!" the girl retorted defiantly, guessing why Nancy had come. "The gypsies have promised to get me into films!"

"Please don't believe them! If they did that, it wouldn't be for years and years, anyway."

Rose started to argue. Nancy knew precious time was being lost.

"Rose, have you met your father yet?" she asked to divert the girl's mind.

"My father?" Rose's face was a blank. "No! Is he here?" She raised her voice alarmingly.

"Sh!" Nancy warned. "Yes, he's here, and I believe he might leave with us. Come, we'll find him."

Making sure that no one would see them, Nancy took Rose's hand and they darted out of the tent to the one Romano had entered.

Nancy peered inside. The gypsy violinist sat on a bed, his head resting dejectedly on his hands.

"Mr Pepito!" she whispered, entering with Rose and closing the tent flap. "I have brought your daughter!"

The man's head jerked up in fright. He stared first at Nancy, then at Rose. As he recognised his daughter, he got to his feet, and with a cry of joy caught her in his arms.

"Rose! My little Rose!" he sobbed. "You are alive and well!"

"Father! Don't ever leave me again!" she pleaded.

"No, you and I will stay together always. No matter what Zorus says, we will go away from the gypsies." Then suddenly recalling that Nancy, a stranger to him and not a gypsy, was standing there, he asked, "Who is this, Rose? A friend of yours?"

"She's Nancy Drew and she's been helping Granny find her stolen dolls."

Instantly a look of alarm crossed Romano's face. "Go at once, Miss Drew!" he cried. "Run! You are in great danger here!"

"From whom?" the girl asked.

"I cannot tell you."

"If I go, Rose goes with me."

"Oh, no, please. I have nothing to live for but my daughter."

"Why don't you both go to Mrs Struthers?" Nancy argued. "She wants you and needs you."

"Never!"

"She has forgiven you for everything, and wants both you and Rose to be with her. Besides," Nancy added practically, "then you can use the money you earn for them and stop giving it to Zorus."

Romano blanched. "You know——"

"About the Cause, and Anton and Nitaka. Tell me, why was Rose brought here?"

Before the man could answer, there came a shout from outside. Romano turned deathly white. "If we're caught ——" He looked appealingly at Nancy.

"Please follow what I tell you both to do," she said quickly. "Mr Pepito, you stay here until I come back."

She seized Rose's hand, and the two girls slid underneath the back of the tent.

"Now go to your own tent," Nancy instructed Rose. "Act as if nothing had happened."

"Where are you going, Nancy?" she cried in fright.

"To hide until I can make some plans."

Nancy dodged along behind the row of tents until she came to one from which she could hear no voices. Taking a chance that it was vacant, she crawled inside. No one was there. The tent was attractively furnished with handmade rugs and silken hangings.

A blanket thrown over a bed caught her eye. It was a duplicate of the one which had been sent to her! But the warning words were missing and also the name, H. Bostwick.

"Maybe this is Henrietta Bostwick's tent," the girl thought excitedly. "Who is she, I wonder?"

In a corner of the tent stood a trunk. As she wondered if any stolen property might be hidden in it, the girl heard footsteps outside. She quickly hid behind one of the silken draperies.

A woman Nancy had never seen came in. She went at once to the trunk, unlocked it, and from its depths removed two dolls: one was Enid Struthers' childhood toy; the other was dressed in bridal garments.

"That bride is the doll I'm looking for!" thought Nancy wildly, gazing at the lifelike figure of Enid Struthers.

The woman carefully placed the dolls on the nearby bed. Turning, she left the tent. Quick as a flash, Nancy came out of hiding. She snatched up the bridal doll, and then in shocked surprise almost let it fall from her hand.

The figure was as warm as a human being!

· 24 ·   *The Mad King*

HER momentary fright gone, Nancy stood lost in thought.

"At last I've found the doll for Rose!" she said to herself. "And I believe I've guessed its secret," she thought excitedly, holding the warm object and examining it. "There's something inside it which has the same energy-giving effect as 'the source of light'. Some kind of ray, some . . ."

"So!" said an icy voice behind her. "Nancy Drew has learned our secret!"

Nancy whirled to face Nitaka! But the gypsy was not the neatly dressed, tailored woman she had seen on previous occasions. She had carelessly thrown on a gaudy robe and her uncombed hair stood out from her head like a wild animal's.

The girl before her, still holding the bridal figure of Enid Struthers, showed no fear, though her pulse quickened. "Yes, I have learned your secret," she answered steadily. "Now I will go and return this stolen property to its rightful owner."

"The secret belongs to us gypsies!" cried Nitaka. "No one can take it from us! Put that down!"

"This doll belongs to the daughter of a gypsy," Nancy countered.

"You mean Rose?" Nitaka laughed wickedly. "She will not need it now. That child will be too busy getting ready for her film career. Then when her grandmother dies . . ."

As Nancy gasped in horror, the woman added quickly,

145

"Oh, we shall not harm Mrs Struthers. But she is old, and as soon as she learns Rose is gone from her forever, she will die of a broken heart."

"Then what will happen?" Nancy asked.

She felt very calm now and sufficiently invigorated to carry on a battle of wits against this woman and all her other gypsy enemies as well. Was it a fantastic idea, or was Nancy's strength being renewed by the substance inside the figure in her arms? Nitaka seemed to sense her thoughts, for she cried:

"Put down that doll!"

Nancy paid no attention. Yet she must play for time until her father could get there. It would take him over two hours to reach the camp.

Then a sinking sensation hit Nancy. Possibly the sleepy cab driver had forgotten to telephone him! Bess and George? Nancy almost hoped they would not find her. She had a strong hunch that the gypsies would not let her go, and if the cousins should come, they might find themselves in the same predicament.

Again Nitaka seemed to read Nancy's mind. "Anyone who gets into the clutches of the great Zorus never leaves," she said, looking at the girl. "You are a prisoner, and if you value your life you will work for the Cause . . . and gladly!"

"That is how you get your money, isn't it?" asked Nancy. "By threats. But your game is up, Nitaka. You and Anton and Tony Wassell have stolen all the jewels and valuable objects you are going to!"

Nitaka, her eyes ablaze, sprang forward. The enraged woman's fingers reached out for Nancy like grasping claws. Dodging, she made a dash for the canvas flap of the tent. The gypsy cried out:

"Anton! Anton!"

The man rushed into the tent and barred the exit. Nitaka said a few frenzied words to him in Romany, including the name Tony, and hurried outside. Anton smiled evilly at Nancy.

"You will be a pretty addition to our tribe, and a clever one," he said ingratiatingly. "Nitaka has gone to get our king. He will decide what work you will do."

A moment later, old Zorus in his regal robes pushed aside the tent flap and entered. Nitaka followed.

"Ha! You catch this spy at last!" the gypsy cried. "But with this girl one of our caravan, our path will be smooth once more."

He spoke in Romany for several seconds, shaking his head so violently, his long white hair waved to and fro. Then, looking directly at Nancy again, his eyes narrow and calculating, he said gloatingly:

"A few more years and gypsies will become all-powerful. King Zorus will reign in America, and Anton and Nitaka shall be Prince and Princess of all the people!"

Nancy looked at his gleaming eyes and knew that the man was quite mad. Undoubtedly he had held sway over his people through promises of riches and power if they obeyed, and threats to their lives if they refused.

What was she to do? Try as she did to calm the three gypsies, her words had no effect. Suddenly Zorus raised his arm in command.

"We go. I do not trust this girl. Her friends may come." More words in Romany, then, "Where we go, she never will be found. Get the tents! Pack the wagons! Two cars will go ahead to the mountain hide-out. In them will be the three we do not want the police to see!" He gave a laugh that sent a chill down Nancy's spine.

Then he gave further instructions in Romany, and left the tent with Anton. Nitaka grabbed the doll, told Nancy not to dare leave, and went outside. For a brief instant she thought she might escape. She looked beneath all the sides of the canvas, but realised it was completely surrounded by Zorus's loyal henchmen.

As Nancy's hopes of help from her father faded, a woman quietly entered the tent. She looked vaguely familiar.

"Have no fear of me," she whispered. "I'm a friend. Once, when I heard Zorus say Anton and Nitaka were in New York and were going to send you a wicked present, I went to Hillcrest and telephoned you a warning."

"The doll with the sleeping drug in it?"

"Yes. And after you met Murko, I sent a blanket with a message. I was afraid for you."

"And you tried to help me when I came to your camp on the river with two girls," Nancy recalled, now recognizing the woman. "You gave me the clue about 'gypsy music fills the air'! But who are you?"

"Can't you guess?"

"Henrietta Bostwick! But that's not a gypsy name."

The woman nodded. "Old Zorus believes me to be one, though. He does not know my maiden name. That was why I left it on the blanket. He thinks that blanket was stolen and that pleases him."

"Why do you stay here?" Nancy asked in a low voice.

"When I was young I ran away to marry a gypsy," the woman explained. "I had to be one of them in order to stay with my husband. I darkened my skin and learned the Romany language so his people thought I came from another tribe. When he died, I wanted to run away, but I was afraid. Most gypsies are fine people, but there are evil members in this tribe and they steal from the others. Whenever Zorus and his helpers plan to harm anyone, I do my best to warn them as I did you."

Nancy told the woman about finding an album in New York bearing her name, and of the help it had been in piecing bits of the puzzle together because of the "source of light" quotation in it.

"Oh, I wrote that in there one day when I heard Nitaka say it. The album was my mother's. I kept it with me always," Henrietta Bostwick said. "But it disappeared and I believe it was sold by Nitaka." She was silent a moment, apparently remembering happier days. Then she added, "I will help you now if I can, but we must be very careful. Zorus has ordered this tent watched. I dare remain only a moment."

"Before you go, tell me about the doll," Nancy asked.

The woman came very close to the girl, and spoke so softly she could hardly hear her. "Some years ago Romano's father found a strange substance at faraway Bear Claw Mountain. Though he was old and infirm, he seemed to feel better whenever he carried it with him. He never told anyone about it except Romano and Zorus.

"When he was about to die, he gave it to Romano. It was at that time Romano married and was banished. Seven years later, Zorus became leader. He had a mad idea of becoming king of America and wanted to live forever. But Romano would not give him the curative substance, nor would he tell where it was. Finally Zorus had him kidnapped, but still he would say nothing. He has been held ever since by Zorus, under the threat that his wife and child would be harmed if he did not stay with the king and work for him."

"And no doubt Enid assumed he had left her," surmised Nancy. "Romano has brought a lot of money to the tribe, hasn't he?"

"Not to the tribe. To Zorus. The king takes everything. He is very clever. It was not until Zorus learned Enid Struthers had died that he sent Romano out to play the violin. By that time Romano had no idea where his daughter was and Zorus would not tell him."

"But it was because of the threat to Rose's life that he stayed with the tribe?"

"Yes. Yet recently he kept saying he was going to leave, and finally Zorus demanded that Rose be brought here to keep him happy. You were responsible for keeping her away until now. You know she's here, don't you?"

"That's one reason I came," said Nancy. "Tell me, how

did Zorus find out where Romano had hidden the strange substance?"

"Quite by accident. He sent Nitaka to Enid Struthers with a forged note from Romano that he wanted to come back to his wife. In proof of her desire to see him, Enid was to send him the precious substance. Enid then gave her the doll. Oh, Nitaka is clever, but wicked."

A voice from outside the tent gave sudden warning that Zorus was returning.

"I must go!" murmured Henrietta Bostwick, raising the back tent flap.

Barely had the woman disappeared than Zorus and four other men came in.

"The girl goes in the first car!" ordered the gypsy king. "Next Romano. Then the child."

Struggling, Nancy was carried outside. She was bound and a handkerchief tied across her mouth. Then she was laid on the floor of a waiting lorry, and a blanket thrown over her.

With a sinking heart, Nancy felt the truck begin to move to an unknown destination!

• 25 •   Two Victories

FOR half an hour Nancy was tossed about on the floor of the moving lorry, before she managed to get herself on top of the blanket. But the vibration and the handkerchief across her mouth made her feel quite ill.

"Oh, if Dad only could have reached me in time!" she told herself over and over.

Then suddenly, just as Nancy felt as if she would faint, the lorry halted abruptly. The back door was jerked open suddenly, and a man hopped inside. He was a policeman!

"Here she is!" he cried out, cutting the cords which bound Nancy, and helping the girl to her feet.

Then she saw her father, who lifted her out and clasped her, trembling, in his arms.

"Oh, Dad, I thought you'd never come!" she said, snuggling into his neck. When he finally set her down, she asked, "Did a taxi driver phone you about me?"

"Yes," Mr Drew replied grimly. "When I heard you'd sent for me I had a hunch I'd better move fast. I came by plane, and landed at the Aiken field. On the way I decided I'd better bring the police with me."

"How did you find out where they were taking me?" Nancy asked.

"A Henrietta Bostwick at the camp whispered the secret to me," her father explained.

Nancy told her story to him and the police. As a result, Zorus, Anton, and Nitaka were jailed. Rose and Romano were found and freed, and went with the Drews. In Aiken Nancy stopped to telephone Mrs Struthers that Rose was safe, and to ascertain that Bess and George had abandoned the search for her and were on their way home by train. They had telephoned Mr Drew, only to find he was on his way to assist his daughter.

Rose and her father travelled to River Heights in Nancy's car. The beautiful doll which had caused so much trouble lay in a box beside them on the back seat.

Presently Nancy turned to Romano and said, "Mr Pepito, before your wife passed away she left a request that Mrs Struthers find a certain doll for Rose. Was it the bridal doll, and does it contain an energy-giving substance?"

"It contains a secret substance which I believe has a curative value. I told Enid never to part with the doll, in case there was something commercially valuable to the idea. Music interested me more than business, so I never investigated the matter, nor tried to find any more of the stuff at Bear Claw Mountain. I believe Enid must have felt that there might be a source of income in it for Rose."

To spare the man's feelings, Nancy changed the subject and told Romano about his daughter's talent as a violinist and dancer. Rose, in the back seat with him, had not taken her eyes from her father's face. Subdued by her experience, she seemed to have suddenly become a quiet, well-behaved child.

"You're coming to Granny's with me, aren't you?" she asked him, taking his hand in her own.

"You're sure she wants me to?"

Nancy turned and smiled. "Mrs Struthers told me on the phone she's waiting for you both with open arms."

When they reached the Struthers residence, Rose tried to induce the Drews to come in, but they tactfully refused, and left Romano and his daughter at the gate.

"I'll come to see you in a few days," Nancy told them as she waved goodbye. "I hope to have a surprise for you then. There's still part of the mystery I hope to clear up."

Nancy, after submitting to Hannah Gruen's affectionate care, tumbled into bed and slept for ten hours. When she woke up, she felt completely refreshed. Bess and George arrived just as Nancy was getting out of bed.

"So you finally solved the mystery without us," said George accusingly.

"Tell us all about it," Bess pleaded. "Weren't you scared silly?"

"I'm afraid I was," laughed Nancy, and related the highlights of her capture and release.

"Do you know what day this is?" George asked suddenly

"Regatta day!" Nancy exclaimed after a moment's thought. "How could I forget? But we have no boat to sail in the Dixon cup races."

"That's where you're wrong!" George replied. "Sam

Pickard stayed up all night to get *Whip the Wind* in shape for the race. Bess and I went out with him early this morning, and she handles beautifully!"

"Then we can race against Phyllis and the other girls!"

"We can if you get to the clubhouse in time, Nancy. The race is set for two o'clock, and we ought to give her a trial run first."

Spurred to action, Nancy got dressed quickly and the girls hurried to the yacht club. There they changed into slacks, shirts and rubber-soled shoes. The sail was hoisted. Five minutes later the sailors leaped into *Whip the Wind* and Nancy took the helm.

"Oh, the boat's wonderful!" she exclaimed, when they had gone half a mile and come about. "Better than before the hole was put in her prow."

The girls barely had time to go over the first leg of the course when all the boats were ordered in so that the junior boys' race could start.

"We made wonderful time," said George enthusiastically. "If we can only do as well in the race . . ."

Two o'clock seemed to arrive in no time and the three girls climbed aboard *Whip the Wind* again, their hopes high.

"The flag has gone up!" George warned nervously. "We'd better work our way over to the starting line."

"We'll make it," Nancy said calmly, her eye on the sail. "Look at our pennant!" cried George. "What a wind!"

The race was to be over a triangular course which the girls now knew by heart. The competition would be stiff because several of the small craft were of the latest design and many were being handled by experienced sailors. Nancy and her friends were fully aware of the skill they must use if they were to win the race.

"There goes the gun!" yelled George.

With clever manoeuvering on Nancy's part and some luck, *Whip the Wind* was the first boat over the starting line. Sailing before the wind, she cut through the water at a fast clip, fully three lengths ahead of her nearest rival. Nancy made every effort to hold her lead, crying out for Bess and George to shift their weight to the stern to keep the boat from nosing over.

"We're still ahead!" yelled George, then the words died in her throat.

Near the first turn, *Whip the Wind* had struck a bad crosscurrent which swung her wide of the course. Phyllis Bean and her friends in the *Lass*, who had been gradually pulling up on Nancy, now sped past. Nancy steadied *Whip the Wind*, but as the two boats rounded Star Island, Phyllis was in the lead by several lengths.

George and Bess were frantic as they started the second leg, which was only a mile long. Try as they might to overtake the *Lass*, the girls did not succeed. Phyllis Bean still held first place!

"Oh, Nancy, I'd just hate to see that conceited girl win," wailed Bess.

"She won't!" roared George. "Come on, Nancy, let's show her what we've got!"

Grim and determined, Nancy realised they faced the hardest test yet. In the final leg, which was about five miles long, they would have to beat to windward all the way to the clubhouse.

Nancy started tacking, her heart in her throat. Her pulse drummed a sing-song rhythm of "Steady on your course, steady on your course!"

As she cleverly zig-zagged to take advantage of every bit of wind, she kept talking encouragingly to *Whip the Wind*. The little boat seemed to catch the spirit to win, her sharp lines cutting through the water with tremendous energy. A quarter of a mile from the clubhouse, they passed Phyllis's boat!

Now there was no holding her. On and on she rushed. Then, amid uncontrollable shouts from George, *Whip the*

Wind shot over the finishing line several lengths ahead of the *Lass*.

"We've won! We've won!" screamed Bess, waving her arms wildly.

Horns began to toot. As the boat docked, the three girls were heartily congratulated and later presented with a silver loving cup. The yacht-club president announced the speed in the young women's race had broken the record for that distance. Nancy and her crew took the acclaim modestly, and then Nancy escaped from the festivities to attend to the final details of the Struthers mystery.

Three days later, she, Bess and George drove to the big brick mansion. Nancy felt satisfied. Tony Wassell, the last of the crooks to confess, had broken down that morning and owned up to all Nancy's accusations.

In the car with the girls was a woman whom no one would have recognised. She was quietly and becomingly dressed. Her hair was newly arranged and her skin soft and white.

"Nancy, I wonder if Romano will know me," she said as the car stopped. "Oh, I'm so happy, and so indebted to you. I can hardly wait to start the job you got me at the hand-woven blanket shop in town. Here comes Rose," she added, as she saw the girl skipping down the front path to meet them.

"The most wonderful thing has happened, Nancy!" Rose cried out. "My father saw his friend Alfred Blackwell, and he listened to me play. He fixed it so Dad and I are going to be together in films!"

"That's wonderful!" Nancy smiled, giving the girl a hug and introducing the woman with her. "This is Mrs Bostwick. And here are all the stolen dolls," she added, handing Rose a package the police had given Nancy. "Suppose you put them in place for your grandmother."

In the house Mrs Struthers was talking happily to her son-in-law. She greeted the callers effusively, while Romano gazed unbelievingly at the transformation in the erstwhile gypsy woman, Henrietta Bostwick.

"We owe so much to Nancy," he said. "We can never repay her."

"Perhaps we can a little bit," said Mrs Struthers. "Nancy, did you bring . . . ?"

From her bag the girl took an envelope the police had found at the gypsy camp, and dropped several sparkling gems into her hostess's hand.

"Choose the one you like best for a ring," Mrs Struthers directed.

"Oh, no, please," Nancy pleaded. "My reward is in having everything turn out so well."

"You certainly did a good job, Nancy," Bess spoke up. She began thinking of what Nancy's next case might involve. She would have shuddered had she known of the narrow escape her friend was to have in *The Witch Tree Symbol*.

But at the moment, Nancy, quite unaware of this, said to Mrs Struthers, "These gems belong in the old album. I'd rather put them back there than keep any." She smiled. "Do you know that if Anton had stolen the beautiful old album instead of merely the jewels, I might never have solved the mystery?"

"If you hadn't used the clue in it of the photograph, you would have solved the mystery with the 'source of light' note," said George loyally. "By the way, who wrote that note?"

"Nitaka sent it to Rose's mother after she took the doll," Nancy explained. "It was to notify her that the doll would not be returned."

Nancy had brought along a pair of jewellers' pliers and as she prepared to put the gems back into the filigree work, Mrs Struthers said:

"Nancy, I insist you have at least a keepsake to remind you of this mystery. Would you like one of the dolls?"

"Oh, don't give her that wicked sword doll!" exclaimed Rose.

"No," laughed Mrs Struthers. "But perhaps Nancy would like to have the fan doll. Would you, Nancy?"

"I'd love it," exclaimed Nancy. "And I'll treasure it always. Oh," she added, "I have something else for you, Mrs Struthers."

Opening her bag again, Nancy handed over another envelope, rather mussed but with its wax seal unbroken. The woman's eyes filled with tears as she looked at it.

"The photograph and the letter stolen from my hand-bag!" she exclaimed.

"No one has looked at them," smiled Nancy. "Not even Tony, who left them in his suitcase at the gypsy camp and then was caught. So their secret is still yours, Mrs Struthers."

Nancy Drew
Mystery Stories

by Carolyn Keene

Look out for these exciting new titles
available in Armada from your local bookshop
in 1987:

Armada

'JINNY' BOOKS
by Patricia Leitch

When Jinny Manders rescues Shantih, a chestnut Arab, from a cruel circus, her dreams of owning a horse of her own seem to come true. But Shantih is wild and unrideable.

This is an exciting and moving series of books about a very special relationship between a girl and a magnificent horse.

Armada

The Chalet School Series
by Elinor M. Brent-Dyer

Elinor M. Brent-Dyer has written many books about life at the famous Alpine school. Follow the thrilling adventures of Joey, Mary-Lou and all the other well-loved characters in this delightful school series.

Below is a list of Chalet School titles available in Armada. Have you read them all?